Philip José Farmer was born in 1918. A part-time student at Bradley University, he gained a BA in English in 1950. Two years later he shocked the sf world with the publication of his novella *The Lovers* in *Startling Stories*. This won him a Hugo Award in 1953; his second Hugo came in 1968 for the story *Riders of the Purple Wage* written for Harlan Ellison's famous *Dangerous Visions* series; and his third came in 1972 for the first part of the acclaimed Riverworld series, *To Your Scattered Bodies Go*. Leslie Fiedler, eminent critic and Professor of English at the State University of New York at Buffalo, has said that Farmer 'has an imagination capable of being kindled by the irredeemable mystery of the universe and of the soul, and in turn able to kindle the imagination of others – readers who for a couple of generations have been turning to science fiction to keep wonder and ecstasy alive'. Philip José Farmer lives and works in Peoria, Illinois.

By the same author

*The Lovers*
*Doc Savage: His Apocalyptic Life*
*Lord Tyger*
*Strange Relations*
*Tarzan Alive*
*Time's Last Gift*
*Traitor to the Living*
*The Stone God Awakens*
*Flesh*
*Behind the Walls of Terra*
*The Image of the Beast*
*A Feast Unknown*
*The Gates of Creation*
*The Maker of Universes*
*Night of Light*
*A Private Cosmos*
*The Wind Whales of Ishmael*
*The Lavalite World*
*Jesus on Mars*
*Dark is the Sun*
*The Unreasoning Mask*
*The Book of Philip José Farmer*

The *Riverworld* Series
*To Your Scattered Bodies Go*
*The Fabulous Riverboat*
*The Dark Design*
*The Magic Labyrinth*
*Gods of Riverworld*

*Riverworld and Other Stories*

# PHILIP JOSÉ FARMER

# Blown

or Sketches Among the Ruins of My Mind
An Exorcism: Ritual Two

PANTHER
Granada Publishing

Panther Books
Granada Publishing Ltd
8 Grafton Street, London W1X 3LA

Published by Panther Books 1985

First published in Great Britain by
Quartet Books Limited 1975

Copyright © Philip José Farmer 1969

ISBN 0-586-06211-4

Printed and bound in Great Britain by
Collins, Glasgow

Set in Baskerville

# 1

It seemed that the rain would never stop.

On the evening of the sixth day, in a city like the planet of Venus in a 1932 science-fiction story, Herald Childe followed Vivienne Mabcrough.

A few minutes before, he had stopped behind a big black Rolls-Royce, waiting for a light change at the intersection of Santa Monica Boulevard and Canon Drive in Beverly Hills. The Rolls was equipped with rear window wipers, and these enabled Childe to see Vivienne Mabcrough.

She was in the back seat with a man and turned her head just as the light changed to green. Childe would never forget that profile. It was not only the most beautiful he had ever seen, but the last time he had seen it, he had been in a situation he would like to forget but could not.

For several seconds, while horns blared behind him, he had an impulse to let her go. If he trailed her, he might find himself the object of attention from her and her kind. And that was something no sane man and very few insane would wish.

Despite this, he moved the 1972 Pontiac across the street after the Rolls, cutting off a Jaguar which had swung illegally to his left to pass him. The Jaguar's horn blared, and the driver mouthed curses behind his glass and plastic enclosure. A spray of water covered Childe's car, and then the wipers removed it. He could see the Rolls turn west on Little Santa Monica, going through a yellow light. He stopped for the red and, seeing no police car in any direction – though he could not see far because of the gray curtains of water – he went left on the red light. He saw the taillights of the Rolls turn right and followed. The Rolls was stopped before the Moonlark Restaurant, and Vivienne and her escort were getting out. They only had to take one step to be under the canopy and a doorman assisted them. The Rolls drove off then, and Childe decided to follow it. The driver was a uniformed chauffeur, and possibly he would take the car back to Vivienne's residence. Of course, the car could be her partner's, but that did not matter. Childe wanted to know where he lived, too.

Although he was no longer a private detective, Childe had kept his recording equipment in the car. He described the car and the license plate number into the microphone while he tracked it back across Santa Monica and then north of Sunset Boulevard. The car swung on to Lexington, and in two blocks drove on to the circular driveway before a huge Georgian mansion. The chauffeur got out and went down the walk along the side of the house to the rear. Childe drove half a block and then got out and walked back. The rain and the dusky light made it impossible for him to see any house addresses from the street. He had to go up the driveway, hoping that no one would look out. The house was lit within, but he could see no sign of life.

He returned to the car, which he entered on the right side because he did not wish to wet his shoes and legs. The dirty gray-brown water had filled the street from curb to curb and was running over on to the strips of grass between street and sidewalk.

In the car, he recorded the address. But instead of driving off, he sat for a long time and considered what he should do next.

They had not bothered him since that night in Baron Igescu's house, so why should he bother them?

They were murderers, torturers, abductors. He knew this with the certainty of personal experience. Yet he could not prove what he knew. And if he told exactly what had happened, he would be committed to a mental institution. Moreover, he could not blame the authorities for putting him away.

There were times when he could not believe his own vivid memories. Even the most piercing, that of the time when he had flushed the complete skin of Dolores del Osorojo, eyes and all, down the toilet, was beginning to seem unbelievable.

The mind accepted certain forms and categories, and his experiences with Igescu, Vivienne Mabcrough, Standing Grass, Fred Pao, and others in that enormous old house in northern Beverly Hills were outside the accepted. And so it had been natural that his mind should be busy trying to bury these forms and categories. Shove them down, choke them off in the dusty dusky cellar of the unconscious.

He could just go home to his place in Topanga Canyon and forget all about this, or try to.

He groaned. He was hooked and couldn't fight loose. He had always wondered about the true identity of Igescu and his people. Were they really vampires, werewolves, werebears, werefoxes, and

6

other creatures which mankind generally considered only to be superstitions? Even Igescu's seemingly 'scientific' account of their origins and nature, which were detailed by the old French scholar Le Garrault, now sounded outrageous. But Igescu's explanation was better than just superstition.

He groaned again and then swore. He was going to pursue this. If he had not seen Vivienne, he might have continued to ignore his desires to take up the trail once more. But the sight of her had gotten him as eager as an old bloodhound that smells a whiff of fox on the wind from the hills.

He drove away and did not stop until he pulled into a Santa Monica service station. There was a public phone booth here, which he used to call the Los Angeles Police Department. His friend, Sergeant Furr, finally answered. Childe asked him to check out the license number of the Rolls. Furr said he would call him back within a few minutes. Three minutes later, the phone in the booth rang.

'Hal? I got it for you. The Rolls belongs to a Mrs Vivienne – V-I-V-I-E-N-N-E – Mabcrough. I don't know how you pronounce that last name. M-A-B-C-R-O-U-G-H. Mabcrow? Mabcruff? I dunno. Anyway . . .'

The address was that of the house where the Rolls was parked.

Childe thanked Furr and hung up. Vivienne was confident that he would not bother her anymore. Even after she had been in conspiracy to kill him, and after he knew that she had killed his partner by biting his penis off, she had not changed her name. Evidently she believed that he had had such a scare thrown into him, he would under no circumstances come near her or her kind – whatever that was.

He trudged through the rain and got into the car and drove slowly and carefully back to the house in which Vivienne Mabcrough lived. It was nightfall now, and the streets of Beverly Hills in the downtown district were little rivers, curb to curb and overflowing. Although this was a Thursday night, there were very few pedestrians out. The usual bumper to bumper traffic was missing. Not half a dozen cars were in sight within the distance of three blocks in any direction. Santa Monica Boulevard traffic was heavier, because it served as a main avenue for those on their way to Westwood or West Los Angeles or Santa Monica on one side of the street, and on their way to Los Angeles, or parts of Beverly Hills, on the other.

The headlights looked like the eyes of diluvian monsters burning with a fever to get on the Ark. A car had stalled as it was halfway through making a left turn from Santa Monica on to Beverly Drive, and the monsters were blaring or hooting at it. Childe nudged his car through the intersection, taking two changes of light to do so because cars in the lanes at right angles insisted on coming through instead of waiting so that the intersection could be cleared.

When he got through, he proceeded up Beverly Drive at about twenty miles an hour but slowed down to fifteen after several blocks. The water was so high that he was afraid of drowning out his motor, and his brakes were getting wet. He kept applying a little pressure intermittently to the pedal in order to keep the brakes dry, but he did not think he was having much success. Four cars went by him, passing from behind or going the other way, and these traveled so fast they threw water all over his car. He wanted to stick his head out of the window and curse at them for their stupidity and general swinishness, but he did not care to be drenched by the next car.

He parked half a block down from the Mabcrough residence. Hours passed. He was impatient at first, and then the habits of years of sitting and waiting while he was a private eye locked into his nervous system. He pissed a couple of times into a device much like airplane pilots use. He munched on some crackers and a stick of beef jerky and drank some coffee from a canteen. Midnight came, and his patience was beginning to thin out against the grindstone of time. His nerves were jumping, and he was about to surrender to them.

Then the chauffeur came out from behind the house, got into the Rolls, and drove off. Childe could see the dark figure, outlined by the lights from within the house. He wore a slicker and a shiny transparent covering over his cap. As the car went by, Childe hunkered down behind the wheel. He waited until it was a block away and then swung out to follow it without turning his lights on immediately. The rain had not ceased, and the streets were even deeper in water.

The Rolls picked up Vivienne and her escort at the club and then went back towards the mansion. Childe had hoped it would; he did not feel like trailing her from one spot to another. The Rolls stopped before the big porch to let its passengers off, and they went into the house. The chauffeur drove the car away, presumably to the side entrance and into the garage behind the house. Childe had gotten out of the car by then and walked down along the side of the house.

He saw the lights in the story above the garage come on. The chauffeur, he hoped, lived there.

He went to the side door, which was surrounded by dense shrubbery and a wall behind him. The people next door could not see him, and anybody passing by on the street would not be likely to see him.

The door opened after a few minutes of trying a number of keys. He shot his flashlight around, looking for evidences of a burglar alarm and could not find any. He went on slowly into the house, ready to run if a dog gave warning. There was no sound except the chiming of a big grandfather clock on the second floor.

A moment later, he was crouched outside the partly opened door of Vivienne's bedroom.

# 2

The room was very large. There was a single light on, coming from the lamp which rested on the floor. Its base was at least four feet high and was some red-shot quartz-like stone sculptured into two naked nymphs – or female satyrs – back to back. The shade looked like thin parchment. Childe, seeing this, was chilled through as if a huge icicle had been shoved up his anus all the way to his hindbrain. He remembered the many skins of human beings he had found inside a drawer in a room in Igescu's house. These had been stripped from the corpses – or perhaps the living owners – and resewn so that they could be blown up like balloons.

There were paintings in red, blue, and purple on the lampshade, outlines of semihuman figures writhing in flames.

The walls were covered with what looked like heavy quiltwork. This had three figures, repeated over and over. There was a satyr standing on a low stone on one hoof, the other slightly raised. His back was arched and his arms and head were raised while he blew a syrinx. A nymph was crouched before him sucking on an enormous purple penis. Behind her was a half-human, half-snake creature. Its lower part was that of a gargantuan python with white and purple markings, and the upper part was a woman's from the belly button up. She had full and well-shaped breasts with spearpoint scarlet nipples, a lovely three-cornered face and long silver hair. Her slender fingers were spreading the egg-shaped buttocks of the nymph, who was bent over, and a long forked tongue was issuing from the snake-woman's mouth and just about to enter the anus or the vagina of the nymph.

Beyond the lamp was a tremendous twelve-postered bed with a crimson many-tasseled canopy. On it were Vivienne and the man, both naked.

She was on her back and he was on top with her legs over his shoulders. He was just about to insert his cock.

Childe watched. He expected either something strange coming from the man or something strange, but not unfamiliar, from the woman. When he had been prowling the secret tunnels between the walls of the Igescu mansion, he had seen her in her bedroom. She had thought she was alone, and she had made love to herself in the most outré fashion. He would never forget that.

'Put it in for me, baby,' the man said. He was about thirty-five, dark and hairy and beginning to flesh out.

And then the man screamed and soared backwards off the bed, propelled by his sudden movement and his push upwards with one arm and by a snapping movement of his body that could only have been induced by utmost terror.

He went back and up, trying to stand up at the same time that he moved away from Vivienne. Her legs flew apart as if they were two white birds that had startled each other.

The man fell off the bed and crashed on to the floor. By then, he had quit screaming, but he shook and moaned.

Vivienne got on to her knees and crawled over to look over the edge of the bed at him. Something long and dark-headed between her legs slid back into the slit and disappeared.

'What's the matter, Bill?' she said, looking down at him. 'Did the cat get your cock?'

He was sitting up by then, intently handling and eyeing his penis. He looked up at her with surprise.

'My God! What happened? You ask what happened? I thought . . . I really did think . . . you got teeth in your cunt?'

He stood up. The gray of his skin was beginning to redden out. He waved his prick at her.

'Look at that! There are teethmarks there!'

She took the limp organ, which looked like a giant but sick worm, and bent over to examine it.

'How can you say those are teeth marks?' she said. 'There are some tiny little indentations there, but nothing serious. There! Does that make Mommy's boy feel better?'

She had kissed the big purple-red glans then run her tongue along the shaft.

He backed away, saying, 'Keep your distance, woman!'

'Are you out of your mind?' she said. She was sitting up on the edge of the bed with the magnificently full and conical breasts pointed at him. Her pubis was a large triangle of thick dark-red hair, almost the same shade as the long thick rich auburn hair on her head. The legs were extraordinarily long and very white.

11

Bill continued to keep his distance. He said, 'I tell you; something bit me. You got teeth in your cunt!'

She lay back down on the bed with her legs stretched out so that the tips of her toes touched the floor. She said, 'Put your finger in, darling, and find out what a fool you are.'

He eyed the reddish fleece and the slit, somewhat opened by the posture.

He said, 'I like my finger, too!'

Vivienne sat up suddenly, her beautiful face twisted. 'You asshole! I thought you were a normal healthy man! I didn't know you were psychotic! Teeth in my cunt, indeed! Get to hell out of here before I call the men from the psycho ward!'

Bill looked as if he felt foolish. He said, 'Honest to God, I don't know how to explain it! Maybe I am going nuts! Or maybe I just had a sudden strain, maybe that was the burning sensation I felt! No, by God, it felt like tiny teeth! Or a bunch of needles!'

Vivienne got down off the bed and reached out a hand to Bill.

'Come here, baby. Sit down on the bed. Here!' She patted the edge of the bed.

Bill must have decided that he was making a fool of himself. Moreover, the sight of the superbly shaped Vivienne, with her outrageously beautiful face, overcame his fears. His penis began to swell, but it did not rise. He seated himself on the bed, and Vivienne walked around the side and got a pillow. Returning, she threw it on the floor and got down on her knees on it.

'I've got teeth in my mouth, baby, but I know how to use them,' she said. She picked up the semi-flaccid organ and ran her tongue out to flick the slit on the end of the glans. He jumped a little but settled back to look down at her while she took half of the cock into her mouth. She began to work her head back and forth, slowly, and the organ disappeared entirely, then emerged slick and shining red as far as the head.

Bill shook and moaned and kept his gaze fixed upon the penis diving in and out of those full red lips. He was evidently getting a heightened ecstacy out of watching his cock pistoning into her mouth.

Herald Childe did not know whether he should stay there or not. He wanted to explore the house for anything he might be able to use for evidence against Vivienne and her partners. If he could find the name and addresses, documents, recordings, films, anything that would tend to prove their criminal activities, he should do it now. Vivienne was occupied, and she was unlikely to notice any noise outside this bedroom

However, he was worried about the man. His behaviour made it evident that he was not aware of Vivienne's peculiarities of physiology or her fatal actions. At least, Childe supposed that they were fatal for others. He had never seen her kill anyone or even harm anyone, but he was certain that she was no different than her monstrous associates.

Bill was an innocent in the sense that he was a victim. He had probably never done anything to offend or hurt Vivienne and her group. He was probably just a pickup, as Childe's partner had been a pickup.

Childe shuddered at the memory of that film that had been shipped to the LAPD by the killers. It had shown his partner being sucked off, as Bill now was. The woman had removed her false teeth and inserted razor-edged iron teeth, and bitten off the end of his partner's cock.

The blood was a crimson fountain that burst out frequently in his visions and his dreams.

Childe decided that he would have to interfere. This meant that he could not prowl around the house now. He would have to make sure the man was safe. And he should do so now. But he could not. He wanted to find out what would happen. He would wait a while and then stop it.

Vivienne abruptly stood up, revealing Bill's red and pulsing beak sticking out at a 45-degree angle.

She said, 'Slide back on to the bed, baby, and lie down.'

Whatever reservations he had about her had diminished with the increase in blood pressure. He moved back and lay down with his head on the pillow while she climbed on to the bed. She mouthed the head of his penis for a minute and then said, 'Bill?'

He was flat on his back, his hands spread out, his face turned upwards. His eyes were open. He did not answer.

'Bill?' she said again, a little louder.

When he did not respond, she crawled down to him and looked into his face. She pinched his cheek and then raked it with her fingernails. Blood flowed from four rows on his flesh, but he did not move. His penis, however, reared up, thick, squat, red-purplish, glistening.

13

Vivienne turned then, and Childe saw the smirk. Whatever she was planning, it was proceeding smoothly.

It was then that he should walk into the room, but he was too fascinated to make his move as yet. Bill seemed to be paralyzed, though how it had happened, Childe could not guess. Not at first. Then he realized that that thing had bitten Bill's peter with poisonous teeth. The venom had frozen him, with the exception of his prick. The blood was still pumping into it.

The woman straddled him with the intention of easing down on his cock and letting it slide up into the slit of her vagina. But she only allowed the head to enter and then she stopped descending. She crouched there for about thirty seconds, during which she shook as if she were having an orgasm.

Immediately after, she withdrew, exposing the penis, which was still upright. But there were tiny rills of blood running down its side from several places between the head and the shaft.

Vivienne turned around to straddle him facing away from him. She put her hand below her buttocks to grab the penis and to slide it in again. This time, however, she let her weight slowly down to guide the cock into her anus. And when its head was engulfed, she stopped.

Childe anticipated what would happen next. He felt sick, and he knew he should halt the monstrous rape, but he was also gripped with the desire to witness what, as far as he knew, no man alive had seen. Emphasis on the alive.

Vivienne waited, and then the lips of her slit bulged open. The thick mat of rich red hair was pushed aside, and a tiny head emerged. It was soaked with the lubricating fluids within her cunt, and it had the features of a man. Its hair was black; it had a tiny moustache and goatee; its eyes were two garnets under eyebrows no thicker than the leg of a black widow spider. The lips were so thin as to be invisible; the nose was long and curved.

The head moved forward as the body continued to slide out from the vagina. It raised up on the shaft of the body like a snake, and Childe heard it hiss but knew that that had to be his imagination. It glided on over the wrinkled sac of the testicles and underneath, apparently headed for the anus. Then, it disappeared while the uncoiling body kept issuing from the slit. By then, its head must have gone deep into the man's bowels.

Childe unfroze abruptly. He shook his head as if trying to clear

14

away sleep. He was not sure that he had not fallen into a semihypnotic state while watching the bizarre scene.

He stepped through the door just as Vivienne eased herself down on the penis, driving it all the way up her own anus. Her eyes were closed, and her face was ecstatic. He managed to get close to her while she was moving up and down on the shaft and moaning phrases in a foreign language. The only sounds were her voice, the striking of rain against the windows, and the squeak of the bed springs as she slid up and down on the cock like a monkey on a stick.

Now that he was closer, he could see that the pale and slimy body of the thing was in the man's anus. It apparently had gone in as deeply as it could, or as it cared to, because the motion was stopped. Childe felt sick because he could imagine that golf-sized head with its vicious eyes blind in the night of the bowels and its mouth chewing on whatever it was that it found delectable in there.

# 3

He reached out and touched the pink-red and swollen nipple on that superb breast.

She reacted violently. Her eyes flew open, exposing the beautiful violet, and she rose up off the bed, leaving the throbbing penis sticking up and dragging the body of the thing out of the man's body. Both came loose with a slurping sound, and the tiny mouth of the thing chattered a high-pitched and angry stream of expletives. At least, they sounded like cursing to Childe, although he did not know the language. The words seemed to be Latin in origin; they were vaguely French or perhaps Catalan or something in between.

On seeing Childe, the thing reared up on its body, which coiled behind the head as if it were a rattlesnake. Vivienne continued to move away from Childe, however, retreating to the opposite end of the bed. There she crouched, while the thing swung between her legs and then started to slide back into the vagina. The head was fixed on Childe while this withdrawal occurred. Its red-gleaming eyes were so hateful and deadly that Childe felt as if he had been bitten. Then the head was gone into the slit; the labia closed; it was as if the thing had never existed. Certainly, the thing should *not* exist.

Childe moved up along the bed and reached out and slapped the man in the face. The hand left a red imprint, but that was the only reaction from him. He continued to stare upwards, and his chest rose and fell slowly. His dong was beginning to dwindle and sag.

'That will do no good unless I give him the antidote,' Vivienne said.

Her color was beginning to return, and she was even smiling at him.

'Then give it to him!' Childe said.

'Or you'll do what?'

The tone was not hostile, just questioning.

'I'll call the cops.'

'If you do,' she said evenly, 'you'll be the one hauled away. I'll charge you with breaking and entering, threatened rape, and assault and battery on my friend here and maybe even attempted murder.'

Childe wondered why she would not charge him with actual rape, then it occurred to him that she would not want a physical examination.

He said, 'I'm not in too good a position, it's true. But I don't think you could stand much publicity.'

She climbed down off the bed, brushing against him with one soft hip, and walked to her dresser. She picked up a cigarette, lit it, and then offered him one. He shook his head.

'Then it's a Mexican standoff?' she said.

'Not unless you give this man the antidote,' he said. 'I don't care what it costs me, I'll raise a howl that'll bring this place down around your ears.'

'Very well,' she said.

She opened a drawer while he stood behind her to make sure that there was no weapon in it. She picked up a large sewing needle from a little depression in the top of a block of dark-red wood and walked with it to the man. She inserted its tip into the jugular vein and then walked back to the dresser. By the time she had replaced the needle, Bill was beginning to move his legs and his head. A few minutes later, he groaned and then sat up, his feet on the floor. He looked at the naked Vivienne and at Childe as if he was not sure what was happening.

Childe said, 'Were you conscious?'

Bill nodded. He was concentrating on Vivienne with a peculiar expression.

'I can't believe it!' he said. 'What the hell were you doing with me? You pervert!'

Childe did not understand for a moment. The accusation seemed so mild compared with what had happened. Then he saw that Bill had not witnessed the thing issuing from her vagina. He must have believed that she had stuck some object up his anus.

'Your clothes are over there,' she said, pointing at a chair on the other side of the bed. 'Get dressed and get out.'

Bill stood up unsteadily and walked around the bed. While he dressed clumsily, he said, 'I'll have the cops down here so fast your heads'll swim. *Drugging* me! Drugging *me*! What the hell for? What did you intend to do?'

'I wouldn't call in the cops,' Childe said. 'You heard what she said she'd do. You'd end up with all sorts of charges flung at you, and, believe me, this woman has some powerful connections. Moreover, she is quite capable of murder.'

Bill, looking scared, dressed more swiftly.

Vivienne looked at her wristwatch and said, 'Herald and I have some things we're eager to discuss. Please hurry.'

'Yeah, I'll bet you two perverts do!' Bill said, glaring at both.

'For Christ's sake!' Childe said. 'I saved your life!'

Childe watched Vivienne. She was leaning against the dresser with her weight on one leg, throwing a hip into relief. He hated her. She was so agonizingly beautiful, so desirable. And so coldly fatal, so monstrous, in all senses of that overused and misused word.

Bill finally had his clothes on, except for his raincoat and rubbers. These, Childe supposed, would be in the closet in the vestibule downstairs just off the entrance.

'So long, you queers!' Bill mumbled as he stumbled through the door. 'I'll see you in jail, you can bet on that!'

Vivienne laughed. Childe wondered if he should go with him. Now that he had followed her and was in this den of whatever it was that she and her colleagues were, he wondered if he had made a very wrong decision. It was true he had rescued a victim, but the victim was so stupid he did not realize what he had escaped. Certainly, he did not seem worth the trouble or the risk.

Vivienne waited until the front door loudly slammed. Then she moved slowly towards him, rolling her hips.

He backed away, saying, 'Keep your distance, Vivienne. I have no desire for you; you couldn't possibly seduce me, if that's what you have in mind.'

She laughed again and sat down on the edge of the bed. 'No, of course not! But why are you here? We left you alone, though we could have killed you easily enough at any time. And perhaps we should have, after what you did to us.'

'If you were human, you'd understand why.'

'Oh, you mean the monkey sense of curiosity? Let me remind you of how Malayans catch monkeys. They put food in a jar with a mouth large enough for the monkey to get his paw into but too small for him to withdraw the hand unless he lets loose of the food. Of course, he doesn't let loose, and so the trapper takes him easily.'

'Yes, I know that,' he said. 'Your analogy may be a fairly exact one. I'm here because I still think that your bunch had something to do with my wife's disappearance. I know you denied that, but I can't get it out of my mind that you did away with Sybil. You're

18

certainly capable of doing that. You're capable of anything that's cruel and inhuman.'

'Inhuman?' she said, smiling.

'All right. Point well taken,' he said. 'However, here we are, alone together in this house with no one except Bill knowing that I am here. And he not only does not know who I am, he isn't going to say anything about me. Not after he considers the possible repercussions, especially the fact that he might be suspected.'

'Suspected of what?' she said, her eyes widening. Before he could reply, she said, 'I doubt that he'll say anything to anybody.'

'What do you mean?' he said, although he thought he knew what she was going to say.

She looked at her watch and said, 'He ought to be dying of a heart attack about now.'

She looked up at him and smiled again. 'So pale! So shocked! What did you expect, you babe in the woods? Did you think I'd let him go so he could talk to the police? I could make him regret it, of course, with charges that would put him in jail, but I don't want any publicity whatsoever. Now, really, Herald Childe, how could you be so naive?'

Childe broke loose from the casing of ice that had seemed to be around him. He leaped at her, his hands outstretched, and she tried to roll away from him on the bed to the other side, but he seized her ankle. He dragged her to him, although she slammed one heel into his shoulder. He leaned down between her legs and thrust three fingers into the wet vagina and probed. Something fiery touched one of his fingers, and he knew he had been bitten, but he plunged his hand in as far as he could.

Vivienne screamed with the pain then, but he kept his hand in and, despite the agony of more bites on his other fingers, managed to seize that tiny head. It was slippery, and it resisted, but it came out of her cunt, its mouth working, the minute teeth glittering in the light, its eyes looking like red jewels stuck into its bearded doll face.

He pressed his left shoulder against her right leg to keep it from kicking him and braced his right shoulder against her other leg. She reached down and grabbed his hair and pulled, and the pain was so intense he almost let loose of the thing. But he clung to it and then threw himself backward as hard as he could. The snakelike body shot out from the slit while the tiny mouth screamed like a rabbit dying.

19

As he fell on his back on the floor, he saw the tail slide out of the slit. It came loose much easier than he thought it would. Perhaps he had been wrong in thinking that it was anchored to her in a plexus of flesh.

But there *were* red and bloody roots hanging from the end of the tail, and Vivienne was down on the floor by him writhing and screaming.

He jumped up and threw the thing away. Its slimy muscle-packed body and the grease-soaked head and unadulterated viciousness of the face and eyes were so loathsome he was afraid he was going to vomit.

The body soared across the bed, hit the other edge, flopped, and then slithered off the edge to fall out of sight.

Vivienne quit screaming, though her skin was gray and her eyes were great areas of white with violet islets. She said, 'Now you've done it! I hope I can get back together again!'

He said, 'What?'

He was having difficulty standing. The pain in his fingers was lessening, but that was because a numbness was shooting up his arm and down his side. The room was beginning to be blurred, and Vivienne's white body with the auburn triangle between the legs and torn fleshy roots hanging out of the slit was starting to spin and, at the same time, to recede.

'You wouldn't understand, you stupid human!'

He sank to his knees and then sat down, lowering himself with one arm that threatened to turn into rubber under him. Vivienne's pubis was directly under his eyes, so he saw what was happening despite the increasing fuzziness of vision.

The skin was splitting along the hairline of the pubis. The split became a definite and deep cleavage as if invisible knives were cutting into her and the operators of the knives intended to scoop out the vagina and the womb in one section.

Cracks were appearing across her waist, across her thighs, her knees, her calves, and her feet.

He bent over to see more clearly. There were cracks on her wrists, her elbows, around her breasts, her neck. She looked like a china doll that had fallen on to a cement sidewalk.

When he looked back at her cunt, it had walked out of the space it had occupied between her legs. It was staggering on its own legs, a score or more of needle-thin many-jointed members with a red-flesh

20

color. Its back was the pubis, the rich auburn hair, the slit, and the mound of Venus. Its underside was the protective coating of the vaginal canal. The uterus came next on its many tiny legs, following the vagina as if it hoped to reconnect.

Out from the cavity left by the exodus came other organs, some of which he recognized. That knot and fold of flesh certainly must be the fallopian tube and ovary, and that, what the hell was that?

By then the cleavages around the base of the breasts had met, and the breasts reeled off the steep slope of the ribs and fell down, turning over. One landed on its legs and scuttled off, but the other breast lay on its back – its front, actually – and kicked its many spider legs until it succeeded in getting on its feet – so-called.

The belly had split across and down, as had the upper part of the trunk. The anus and the two cheeks of the buttocks crawled off. The legs of this creature were thicker but the weight of the flesh seemed to be almost too much. It moved slowly, whereas the hands, using the fingers as legs, ran across the room quickly and disappeared under the bed.

The head was also walking towards the underside of the bed. It was lifted off the floor by legs about three inches high and perhaps a sixteenth of an inch thick. Four longer legs that had sprouted from behind her ears supported the head and kept it from falling to one side or another. Vivienne's eyes were wide open and blinking, so that she seemed to be as aware in this state as she was in the other. She did not, however, look at Childe.

He felt sick, but he did not think he was going to vomit. If he was, he could not feel anything churning up. His insides were too numb for anything except a vague feeling of queasiness.

He fell over on his side and could not get up again no matter how hard he struggled. Or tried to struggle, rather, because his efforts were all mental. His muscles, as far as he could tell, failed to respond with even a tremor.

# 4

When he saw the golfball-sized head of the thing poke out from beyond the end of the bed, Childe realized what he had done. By yanking so savagely on that thing, he had jerked it loose from some base in her body, probably in her uterus. This was what he had intended. But he could never have visualized that pulling the thing was like pulling the cord on one of those burro dolls – what were they called? – that were hung up in Mexican homes on Christmas. Pull the string and they ripped open, and all the goodies spilled out.

The thing had been her string, and when it was torn out, she fell apart, and all her goodies, separate entities, spilled out. And began a walk that only a Bosch could paint.

Now the thing was gliding snakelike towards him, its forepart raised off the ground and the slimy, goateed, sharktoothed, scimitar-nosed, garnet-eyed head was pointed at him. Its mouth was writhing, and a piping was issuing from the invisible lips.

Childe could do nothing but lie on his side, his eyes fixed on the approaching thing. He wondered what it had in mind for him. Its bite was poisonous, and while its poison had paralyzed Bill but left his sexual organs active, it might be fatal if he were bitten again. Moreover, Vivienne said an antidote had to be given, and she, as far as he knew, was the only one who could do that. But not while she was in this condition.

A glob of coiled intestines crossed before him, cutting off his view of the snake-thing. Behind it came the spinal area, a flesh centipede. This reeled blindly into a foot, which was traveling upside down, its sole pointed towards the ceiling, while twenty legs bore it to wherever it was going. The spine and the foot fell over on their side and kicked their legs for a while before managing to get back up.

The snake-thing crawled nearer. Childe watched it and speculated on whether or not its underside was equipped with many moving plates to enable it to progress so serpentinely. Did it have an ophidian skeleton?

He was so numb that it did not occur to him to wonder how this whole process could come about. He just accepted it.

Presently, the many-legged cunt, still followed by the many-legged uterus, walked towards him. The hairy-back animal bumped into his stomach, staggered back, half-turned, and bumped along his body. It stopped when it came into contact with his chin, slid along it and around to his mouth, where it stopped. He could not see it, but he had the feeling that it was leaning against his lips. Its hairs brushed his nose and made him sneeze. The odor from it was clean and faintly musky, and under other circumstances he would have enjoyed it very much.

The cunt remained by him, pressing on his mouth, as if it recognized something familiar in its blind and deaf world. The uterus was nestled against his neck, its wet skin on his skin.

The snake-thing kept on coming towards him and then it disappeared around his head. He tried to throw his head back and to turn it, but he could not. Within a few seconds, he felt it crawling up over the back of his head. He wanted to scream, to make a superhuman effort that would enable him to burst out of his own skin and run out of the room. Then the thing was coiled up on his cheek, and the wet beard was tickling the lobe of his ear.

The voice was tiny and tinny.

The words were unintelligible. They were in that same language he had heard before, in between French and Spanish. Like an unnasalized, untruncated French. An archaic French, perhaps.

The tiny tinny voice raged on. Its forked tongue flicked against the inner part of his ear.

Suddenly, there was a silence. The body was still there, but it was motionless. The vagina-thing abruptly scuttled away with the uterus-thing nosing after it. Vivienne's head appeared from under the bed and stalked slowly towards him. Her tongue was sticking out from her lax lips, and her bright eyes stared at him.

Her head stopped a few feet from his eyes. Her eyes looked up, evidently at the thing on his cheek. Her lips moved, but no voice issued. This was to be expected, since she had no lungs. The lungs were twin creatures lurching like sick dinosaurs along a drying swamp towards the far wall.

Maybe, Childe thought, maybe the thing can lip-read. Maybe she's giving him instructions for starting the reassembly process.

But what if there is no reassembly? What if this is final? What do I know about her or others of her kind? All were strange, but some were stranger than others. Vivienne was the strangest. She did not

23

fit into any categories of vampire or werewolf or lamia or ghost. Maybe, when the cord is yanked, the lanyard pulled, she has had it. Surely, she – her parts that is – can't survive long in this condition. They have to eat and to excrete, they are as subject to natural laws as any other creatures, even if they seem to be unnatural.

There is nothing unnatural in this universe. Anything that seems so just isn't explained yet. All things can be explained by natural laws. If you don't know certain laws, then you think a thing is unnatural.

The snake-thing slid down over his eyes on to the floor. It crawled to Vivienne's head and coiled there while the upper part rose to a point a few inches before her eyes. It swayed back and forth like a cobra, and sometimes its head turned. Its mouth was working, and its face was twisted with rage. Only when its head was turned towards him could Childe hear the faint piping voice. It was still using the unknown tongue.

Presently it communicated something or it tired of trying to communicate. It turned and crawled to a point just past his chin. He could not see what it was doing until a moment later. It crawled out past him, towing the uterus behind it. Its tail had been inserted into the interior and probably was being implanted again.

When it was a little distance past his head, it stopped and turned again. It crawled back towards him, stopping with the uterus leaning up against his forehead. The vagina moved away, and he was able to see that the snake-thing was butting it with its head. Herding it.

When it had the vagina maneuvered into the proper position, it slipped through from the rear of the vagina and emerged through the slit. The vagina moved backwards as if impelled by telepathy until it was reunited with the uterus-thing.

Now what? Childe thought, and then he was able to worry about himself for the first time. Maybe the poison did wear off; maybe Vivienne had been lying about the necessity of the antidote. She must have wanted to give Bill an antidote to get him going more quickly. And at the same time she had administered the poison that would stop his heart. If she had not lied about that, of course.

He tried to move but was as unable as before. However, his thinking and his vision were not as unfocused.

Now he began to be impressed with the utter alienness of the life before him. That a living body could fall apart into discrete

24

creatures which were mobile was unthinkable. But there they were. And how did they survive so long? The blood system, for instance, had been cut off, sealed into each creature, but the circulation, of course, had stopped. There was the heart, its veins and arteries closed up, moving away from him towards the underside of the bed on thirty frail legs. Something about it reminded him of a headless chicken.

But how did these things live without the bringing in of oxygen and the carrying away of waste? They had to have some auxiliary source of energy and excretion. Had to have!

And how did Vivienne manage to hide all these fissures and cleavages, all these legs and God knew what other biological mechanisms, in her body? She should have looked fat and lumpy, but she had not. She had a superb body and that face, that painfully beautiful face, now walking around on a score of skinny legs and four support legs from behind her ears!

The snake-thing dragged itself in front of him, trailing the uterus, in chase of the anus and buttocks. Obviously it intended to unite with them. But what then? It was becoming unwieldy and could not corner too many other pieces and unite before it became too heavy and too awkward.

The head had been busy while he watched the snake-thing. It had kicked and pushed the two shoulders until they were huddled together in a corner of the room. Then the head went off in pursuit of various entrail things while the snake-thing backed into the buttocks and anus and hooked up as a railroad engine would hook up several cars with another.

At that moment, he felt the floor vibrate slightly under him. A second later, two large shoes were by his head. Then the shoes moved on out past him, and he saw the chauffeur. He was a big man with a skin as dark as a sunburned Sicilian's, but his features were Baltic. He had a broad face with high cheekbones and a high forehead and straight dark hair. The scene before him did not seem to bother him in the least.

With swift but efficient movements, he began to reassemble Vivienne Mabcrough. The parts were placed together or one inserted into another, and presently she was stretched out on the floor in a unit. The fissures closed; the cracks disappeared; the cleavages filled out. When her skin was again unbroken, he hit her over the heart with his fist. She gasped for air, breathed for a while, and then sat up. She was a little unsteady but waved the hand of the chauffeur away.

The head of the snake-thing came out of her slit and stared angrily at him.

'Barton,' she said, 'put him on the bed and undress him.'

Wordlessly, Barton picked Childe up in his arms and laid him out on the bed. He proceeded to take off all of Childe's clothes and to hang them up neatly in the closet. The shoes and socks went under a chair. Childe could see this because he was able by then to turn his head. He could not, however, talk.

'You can go now, Barton,' Vivienne said.

The big dark man looked emotionlessly at Childe. Then he said, 'Very well, madame,' and left.

Childe wondered what his place was in Vivienne's group. He remembered Glam, the giant servant of Baron Igescu. That man had been a strange one, but he was entirely human, or of human origin anyway. He had made the mistake of falling in love with Magda Holyani, who seemed to be a werepython. She had rejected him, and Glam had tried to rape her. The result: most of his bones broken and his blood and guts squeezed out.

If Barton was wholly of human origin, then he was one of the vilest collaborators in history. Or in unhistory, since history, or any human science or scientific discipline, refused to acknowledge the existence, or the possibility of existence, of these beings.

Vivienne stood over him and bent down so that one breast hung above his mouth a few inches.

She said, 'You frustrated me, my beautiful Herald Childe, and I don't like to be frustrated. You took away my Bill, a stupid ass of a man but a great cock. So you will substitute for him, even though you are now forbidden.'

He wanted to ask what she meant by 'forbidden' but could not even open his mouth.

Vivienne kissed him and thrust her tongue into his mouth and felt his tongue and teeth and gums while she played with his cock with one hand. Despite himself, he responded. His cock felt slightly titillated; it warmed up and swelled a little, if his sense of feel was any indication.

Vivienne moved herself up then and put her nipple in his mouth, but he was unable to suck on it. If he had been able, he would have refused. She was the most beautiful woman he had ever seen, but she was by now far from the most desirable. He did not care for murderesses at all, and he loathed her for that thing coiled in her womb. He hoped it was still coiled there, but he doubted it. His anus was beginning to contract in dread of its coming.

Even though he did not suck or tongue it, her nipple grew large and hard in his mouth. She withdrew it and put the other one between his lips, and it grew large. Then she began to kiss his nipples and to stroke his cheeks with her fingers. She slowly traced her tongue down his belly, working back and forth and across, drawing geometric designs with its tip.

When she came to his pubic hairs, she ran her tongue along the edge of the hairline and then worked her tongue over the hairs until they were wet. His penis swelled some more. He did not want it to be affected in the least by her, but something, perhaps the paralyzing effect of the bite, made him unable to resist. He loathed her and he wanted to scream at the thought of the snake-thing. But the loathing and the horror were numbed, far away. The pleasure of her tongue and lips was the immediate entity.

When he felt her mouth closing around his testicles, he began to be flooded with a hot sensation. It arose from under his navel and spread outwards but chiefly towards the base of his penis. When it oozed into his penis, it filled it out so that it rose up straight and hard.

After a while, she pushed the testicles out with her tongue and lowered her head over his cock. Her lips went softly and wetly around the head, and her tongue pressed against the slit in its end. He groaned deep within himself and could not repress a desire to move his hips upward to drive his prick deeper into her mouth. The desire was all that resulted; his hips remained motionless.

Vivienne continued to suck on the glans and occasionally to move her head down so that the shaft went in all the way. The warmth at the base of his penis became a rod of fire which stretched from the tip of his spine to the tip of his cock. The heavy gray fluid was moving slowly, rubbing against excited nerves, towards the entrance to his shaft.

Suddenly, Vivienne got up and turned around, presenting that lovely back and the egg-shaped buttocks. She squatted over him and reached down and tenderly took the head between her fingers. This she guided into her anus as she lowered herself down on it. The head stuck in the tight mouth for a minute and then abruptly slid in. It moved against a warm slick surface until the flesh of her ass was against his pubic hairs.

She lowered and raised herself slowly several times, causing him to feel ecstatic. It would not take much of this to make him come. And he did not like buggering. Though he had done it several times, in response to women who liked it, he had a distaste for it. Now his repulsion was on the edge of his mind. It bulked large enough for him to be aware of it, but it did not bother him.

She stopped on an upward movement, leaving his cock half in.

Knowing what was about to happen, he mentally gritted his teeth. The horror did not draw any blood from his engorged penis, however.

Suddenly, something slipped down over his testicles. It slid over the sac and under, and something – the thing's bearded little head, of course – touched his anus. Then it entered and was pushing into his anus and then up his rectum. It felt hard and solid and unpleasant, as when a doctor stuck a finger up him for a prostate examination. But this disagreeable sensation did not last long. Something, perhaps its bite or the substance released by its bite, turned unpleasantness into a warm and relaxing feeling.

A few seconds later, Vivienne began to move up and down on his cock, and he could feel the body of the snake-thing sliding back and forth in him. Its motion seemed to be independent of hers; it was moving much faster than her motions could account for.

The warmth and relaxation within his rectum and his bowels gave way to an almost hot feeling and a tension. The tension was, however, near-ecstatic. His insides felt as ready for orgasm as his penis. Both exquisitenesses acted as sine waves out of phase with each other. But as Vivienne increased her slidings up and down his pole, and as the snake-thing continued at the same rapid pace, the waves slowly came into phase.

There was a moment of glory: a flashing red light across his eyes, a spurt of metal rubbing against his pleasure nerves, a breaking through of a red-hot drill in the center of his brain, and he exploded. It was as if he had been turned inside out as he passed through some fifth-dimensional continuum. He was a glove of flesh removed from a hand, inverted, and exposed to radiations.

Vivienne sat on him for a while but rotated on his cock so that she could face him. The action pulled the snake-thing along, but it, apparently, was through. It slid into her slit and out of his anus and

28

then was facing him. Its shaft and head were smeared and it was still expelling a musky gray fluid from its mouth. When the flow had ceased, its forked tongue flickered out and began to clean its face. Within a few minutes, its face and beard looked as if it had showered.

Though it did not look as vicious as before, it still looked dangerous.

Childe was glad to see it withdraw, although he wished that it had not first moved up her body and kissed her on the lower lip with its thin mouth.

Vivienne scooted up when the thing disappeared into her cunt, and his penis slipped out of her anus. She kissed him and said, 'I love you.'

He could not reply, but he thought, 'Love?'

He wished he could vomit.

At that moment, three men entered the room. One of them had a cane, from which he pulled a thin-bladed sword. He stuck the point of it against Vivienne's neck.

She turned pale and said, 'Why are you breaking the truce?'

# 5

Forrest J Ackerman, hiding in the bushes, was getting wetter. He was also becoming madder.

Three days ago he had received through the mail a large flat box. This had come from England, and it contained an original painting by Bram Stoker. The painting depicted Count Dracula in the act of sucking blood from the throat of a young blonde. Many illustrations have done this; a number of reprints of *Dracula*, written by Bram Stoker, have shown Dracula going down on a sleeping young beauty, and innumerable advertisements and stills for various Dracula movies have shown this.

But this was the only painting of Dracula done by the author himself. Until a few months ago, its existence had been unknown. Then a dozen oil paintings and a score of ink drawings had been found in a house in Dublin, once owned by a friend of Stoker's. The present owner had discovered the works in a boarded-up closet in the attic. He had not known what the paintings and drawings represented in money. He had sold them to an art dealer for several pounds and thought himself well ahead.

But the dealer had brought in handwriting experts who verified that the signature on the illustrations was indeed Bram Stoker's. Forry Ackerman, reading of this, had sent a wire to the Dublin art dealer and offered to top any price submitted. The result was that he got his painting but had to go to the bank to get a loan. Since then, he had been waiting anxiously and could talk of little but the expected arrival.

When he unwrapped it, he was not disappointed. Admittedly, Stoker was no St John, Bok, Finlay, or even a Paul. But his work had a certain crude force that a number of people commented upon. It was a primitive, no doubt of that, but a powerful primitive. Forry was glad that it had some artistic merit, although he had no knowledge of what constituted 'good art' and no desire to learn. He knew what he liked, and he liked this.

Besides, even if it had been less powerful, even crude, he would not have cared. He had the *only original painting* of Dracula by the author of *Dracula*. No one else in the world could claim that.

This was no longer true.

That night he had come home to his house in the 800 block of Sherbourne Drive. It was raining then as now, and the water was pouring down his driveway into the street. The street was flooded but the water had not yet risen to cover the sidewalk. It was after one o'clock, and he had just left a party at Wendy's to come here because he had to get out one of his comic magazines. As editor of *Vampirella* and some horror magazines, he had hard schedules to meet. He had to edit *Vampirella* tonight and get it out in the morning, air mail, special delivery, to his publisher in New York.

He had unlocked the door and entered the front room. This was a rather large room decorated with large and small original paintings of science-fiction and fantasy magazine covers, paintings done on commission, stills from various horror and so-called science-fiction movies, photographs of Lon Chaney, Jr as the Wolf Man, Boris Karloff as Boris Karloff, and Bela Lugosi as Dracula. Each bore a signature and a dedication of best wishes and fondest regards to 'Forry.' There were also heads and masks of Frankenstein's monster, the Creature from the Black Lagoon, King Kong, and a number of other fictional monsters. The bookshelves reached from floor to ceiling at several places, and these were jammed with the works of science-fiction authors, Gothic novel writers, and some volumes on exotic sexual practices.

Forry's house had to be seen to be visualized. It had once been his residence, but he had filled it with works evaluated at over a million dollars. He had moved into Wendy's apartment and now used the house as his business office and as his private museum. The day would come – perish the day! – when he would no longer be around to enjoy, to vibrate with joy, in the midst of his dream come true. Then it would become a public museum with the great Ray Bradbury as trustee, and people would come from all over the world to view his collection or to do research in the rare books and with the paintings and manuscripts and letters. He was thinking about having his ashes placed in a bronze bust of Karloff as Frankenstein's monster and the bust put on a pedestal in the middle of this room. Thus he would be here in physical fact, though not in spirit, since he refused to believe in any survival after death.

California law, however, forbade any such deposit of one's ashes.

31

The morticians' and cemetery owners' lobby had ensured that the legislature passed laws beneficial to their interests. Even a man's ashes had to be buried in a cemetery, no matter what his wishes. There was a provision that ashes could be scattered out over the sea, but only from an airplane at a suitable distance and height. And the ashes of only one person at a time could be done so. The lobby ensured that the ashes of a number of deceased were not stored until a mass, thus economical, flight could be made. The lobby ensured that the bereaved made tribute to the jackals of the dead, to the worshippers of Anubis.

Forry, thinking about this, suppressed his anger at the money-hungry and essentially soulless robbers of the bereaved. He wondered if he could not make some arrangements for an illegal placing of his ashes in the bust. Why not? He could get some friends to do it. They were a wild bunch – some of them were – and they would not be stopped by a little illegality.

While he was standing there, taking off his raincoat, he looked around. There was the J. Allen St John painting of Circe and the swine, Ulysses' buddies. And there, pride of his prides, and there . . . and there . . .!

The Stoker was gone.

It had been hung on a place opposite the door so that anybody entering could not miss seeing it. It had displaced two paintings. Forry had had a hard time finding space in this house where every inch of the wall was accounted for.

Now, a blank spot showed where it had been.

Forry crossed the room and sat down. His heart beat only a little faster. He had a faulty pacemaker; it controlled the heart within a narrow range, and that explained why he had to take stairs slowly and could not run. Nor did excitement step up the heart. The emotions were there, however, and they made him quiver when he should have beat.

He thought of calling the police, as he had done several times in the past. His collection had been the object of attentions of many a burglar, usually a science-fiction or horror addict who brushed aside any honesty he might have possessed in his lust to get his hands on books, paintings, stills, manuscripts, masks, photographs of the famous and so forth. He had lost thousands of dollars from this thievery which was bad enough. But the realization that some of the works were irreplaceable hurt him far worse. And the thought that anybody could do these evil things to him, who loved the world as he did not love God, hurt. Who loved people, rather, since he was no Nature lover.

Putting aside his first inclination to call the police, he decided to check with the Dummocks. These were a young couple who had moved in shortly after the previous caretakers, the Wards, had moved out. Lorenzo and Hulia Dummock were broke and houseless, as usual, so he had offered them his hospitality. All they had to do was keep the house clean and fairly well ordered and act as helpers sometimes when he gave a party. Also, they would be his burglar insurance, since he no longer lived in the house.

He went upstairs after calling a number of times and getting no answer. The bedroom was the only room in the house which had space for residents. There was a bed and a dresser and a closet, all of which the Dummocks used. Their clothes were thrown on the bed, the floor, the dresser top, and on a pile of books in one corner. The bed had been unmade for days.

The Dummocks were not there, and he doubted they could be anyplace else in the house. They had gone out for the night, as they quite often did. He did not know where they got their money to spend, since Hulia was the only one working and she did that only between sieges of asthma. Lorenzo wrote stories but had so far been able to sell only his hard-core pornography and not much of that. Forry thought they must be visiting somebody off whom they were undoubtedly sponging. This increased his anger, since he asked very little of them in return for room and board. Being here nights to watch for burglars had been their main job. And if he reproached them for falling down on this, they would sneer at him and accuse him of exploiting them.

He searched through the house and then put on his raincoat and went out to the garage. The Stoker painting was not there.

Five minutes later, he got a phone call. The voice was muffled and unrecognizable, although the caller had identified himself as Rupert Vlad, a friend and a committeeman in the Count Dracula Society. Since Forry took all his calls through the answering service, he could listen in and determine if he wished to answer any. This voice was unfamiliar, but the name got the caller through.

'Forry, this isn't Vlad. Guess you know that?'

'I know,' said Forry softly. 'Who is it?'

'A friend, Forry. You know me, but I'd just as soon not tell you who I really am. I belong to the Lord Ruthven League and the Count Dracula Society, too. I don't want to get anybody mad at me. But I'll tell you something. I heard about you getting that painting of Dracula by Stoker. I was going to come over and see it. But I attended a meeting of the Lord Ruthven League . . . and I saw it there.'

'You what?' Forry said shrilly. For once he had lost his self-control.

'Yeah. I saw it on the wall of, uh, well . . .'

There was a pause.

Forry said, 'For the sake of Hugo, man, don't keep me hanging in air! I have a right to know!'

'Yeah, but I feel such a shit finking on this guy. He . . .'

'He's a thief!' Forry said. 'A terrible thief! You wouldn't be a fink. You'd be doing a public service! Not to mention servicing me!'

Even in his excitement and indignation, he could not keep from punning.

'Yeah, uh, well, I guess you're right. I'll tell you. You go right over to Woolston Heepish's house. You'll see what I'm talking about.'

'Woolston Heepish!' Forry said. He groaned and then added, 'Oh, no!'

'Uh, yeah! I guess he's been bugging you for years, right? I kinda feel sorry for you, Forry, having to put up with him, though I must say he does have a magnificent collection. I guess he should, since he got some of it from you.'

'I never gave him anything!'

'No, but he took. So long, Forry.'

# 6

Fifteen minutes later, Forry was outside the Heepish residence. This was two blocks over from Forry's own house, almost even with it. In the dark and the driving rain, it looked like an exact duplicate of the Ackermansion. It was a California pseudo-Spanish bungalow with a green-painted stucco exterior. The driveway was on the left as you approached the house, and when you stepped past the extension of the house, a wall, you saw the big tree that grew in the patio. It leaned at a forty-five-degree angle across the house, and its branches lay like a great hand over part of the tiled roof. At the end of the driveway was the garage, and in front of the garage was a huge wooden cutout of a movie monster.

You turned to the right and on to a small porch to face a wooden door plastered with various signs: NO SMOKING PERMITTED. WIPE YOUR FEET AND YOUR MIND BEFORE ENTERING. THE EYES OF HEEPISH ARE ON YOU (hinting at the closed-circuit TV with which Heepish scanned his visitors before admitting them). ESPERANTO AND VOLAPUK SPOKEN HERE. (This bugged Forry, who was a long-time and ardent Esperantist. Heepish not only imitated Ackerman with the Esperanto, but, in his efforts to go him one better, had learned Esperanto's closest rival, Volapuk.)

Forry stood for some time before the door, his finger held out to press on the doorbell. The skies were still emptying their bins; the splash of water was all around. Water roared out of the gutter drains and covered the patio. The light above the door gave a ghostly green illumination. All that the scene needed was thunder and lightning, the door swinging open slowly and creakingly, and a tall pale-faced, red-lipped man with sharp features and black hair plastered close to his head, and a deep voice with a Hungarian accent saying, 'Good evening!'

There was no light from the interior of the house. Every window was curtained off or boarded up or barred by bookcases. Forry had not seen the interior of the house, but it had been described to him. His own house was so furnished.

Finally, he dropped his hand from the doorbell. He would scout around a little. After all, he would look like an ass if he barged in demanding to have his painting back, only to find that his informant had lied. It would not be the first time that he had been maliciously misinformed so he would get into an embarrassing situation.

He walked around the side of the house and then to the back. There should be a room here which had once been an anteroom or pantry for the kitchen. In his own house, it was now piled with books and magazines; in fact, he kept his collection of *Doc Savage* magazines just off the kitchen door.

The curtains over the windows were shut tight. He placed his ear against the window in the door but could hear nothing. After a while, he returned to the front. That there were two cars in the driveway and a number parked in the street might indicate that Heepish had guests. Perhaps he should return to his house and phone Heepish.

Then he decided that he would confront Heepish directly. He would not give him a chance to deny he had the painting or to hide it.

Having made up his mind, he still could not bring himself to ring the doorbell. He went to the front of the house and stood in the bushes for a while while the rain pelted him and water dripped off the branches. The confrontation was going to be dreadful. Highly embarrassing. For both of them. Well, maybe not for Heepish. That man had more nerve than a barrel of brass monkeys.

A car passing by threw its water-soaked beams on him for a minute. He blinked against the diffused illumination and then walked from under the shelter of the bush. Why wait any longer? Heepish was not going to come out and invite him in.

He pressed the button, which was the nose of a gargoyle face painted on the door. A loud clanging as of bells came from within followed by several bars of organ music: *Gloomy Sunday*.

There was a peephole in the large door, but Heepish no longer used this, according to Forry's informants. The pressing of the doorbell now activated a TV camera located behind a one-way window on the left of the porch.

A voice from the Frankenstein mask nailed on the door said, 'As I live and don't breathe! Forest J (no period) Ackerman! Thrice welcome!'

A moment later, the door swung open with a loud squeaking as of rusty hinges. This, of course, was a recording synchronized to the door.

Woolston Heepish himself greeted Forry. He was six feet tall, portly, soft-looking, somewhat paunched, and had a prominent dewlap. His walrus moustache was bronzish, and his hair was dark red, straight, and slick. He wore square rimless spectacles behind which gray eyes blinked. He hunched forward as if he had spent most of his life reading books or working at a desk. Or standing under a rainy bush, Forry thought.

'Come in!' he said in a soft voice. He extended a hand which Forry shook, although he wished he could ignore it, let it hang out in the air. But, after all, he did not know for sure that Heepish was guilty.

Then he stiffened, and he dropped Heepish's hand.

Over Heepish's shoulder he saw the painting. It was hung at approximately the same place it had hung in his house. There was Dracula sinking those long canines into the neck of a blonde girl!

He became so angry that the room swirled for a moment.

Heepish took his arm and walked him towards the sofa, saying, 'You look ill, Forry. Surely I don't have *that* effect on you?'

There were five others in the room, and they gathered about the sofa where he sat. They looked handsome and beautiful and were dressed in expensive up-to-the-latest-minute clothes.

'My painting!' Forry gasped. 'The Stoker!'

Heepish looked up at it and put the tips of his fingers together to make a church steeple. He smiled under the walrus moustache.

'You like it! I'm so glad! A fabulous collector's item!'

Forry choked and tried to stand up. One of the guests, a woman who looked as if she were Mexican, pushed him back down.

'You need rest! You look pale. What are you doing out on a night like this? You're soaked! Stay there. I'll get you a cup of coffee.'

'I don't want coffee,' Forry said. He tried to stand up but felt too dizzy. 'I just want my painting back.'

The woman returned with a cup of hot coffee, a package of sugar, and a pitcher of cream on a tray. She offered it to him, saying, 'I am Mrs Panchita Pocyotl.'

'Of course, how graceless of me!' Heepish said. 'I apologize for not introducing you, my dear Forry. My only excuse is that I was worried about your health.'

The other woman was a tall slender blonde with large breasts, a Diana Rumbow. The three men were Fred Pao, a Chinese, Rex Bilgreen, a mulatto, and George Bunyan, an Englishman.

Forry, looking at them clearly for the first time, thought they had something sinister about them. He could not, however, define it.

Maybe it was something about the eyes. Or maybe it was because he was so outraged about the painting he thought that anybody who had anything to do with Heepish was sinister.

Mrs Pocyotl bent over to give him the coffee and exposed large light-chocolate-colored breasts with big red nipples. She wore no brassiere under the thin formal gown with the deep cleavage.

Under other circumstances, he would have been delighted.

Then Diana Rumbow, the blonde, dropped a book she was holding and bent over to pick it up. Despite his upset condition, he responded with a slight popping of the eyes and a stirring around his groin. Her breasts were just as unbrassiered as Panchita's. They were pale white, and the nipples were as large as his thumb tips and so red they must have been rouged. When she stood up, he could see how darkly they stood out under the filmy gown she wore.

He was also beginning to see that the bendings over were not accidents. They were trying to take his mind off his quest.

Pocyotl sat down by him and placed her thigh against his. Diana Rumbow sat down on the other side and leaned her superb breast against the side of his arm. If he looked to either side, he saw swelling mounds and deep cleavages.

'My painting!' he croaked.

Heepish ignored the words. He drew up a chair and sat down facing Forry and said, 'Well! This is a great honor you have done me, Mr Ackerman. Or may I call you Forry?'

'My painting, my Stoker!' Forry croaked again.

'Now that you've finally decided to let bygones be bygones, and, I presume, decided that your hostility towards me was unwarranted, we must talk and talk! We must talk the night out. After all, what with the rain and all, what else is there to do but talk? We have so much in common, so much, as so many people, kind and unkind, have pointed out. I think that we will learn to know each other quite well. Who knows, we might even decide someday that the Count Dracula Society and the Lord Ruthven League can band together, become the Greater Vampire Coven, or something like that, even if witches and not vampires have covens? Heh?'

'My painting,' Forry said.

Heepish continued to talk to him, while the others chattered among themselves. Occasionally, one of the women leaned over against him. He became aware of their perfume, exotic odors that he did not remember ever having smelled before. They stimulated him even in his anger. And those breasts! And Pocyotl's flashing dark eyes and Rumbow's brilliant blue eyes!

He shook his head. What kind of witchcraft were they practicing on him? He had entered with the determination of finding the painting, taking it down from the wall or wherever it was, and marching out the front door with it. Now that he considered that, he would have to find something to protect it from the rain until he could get it into his car, which was across the street. His coat would do it. Never mind that he would get soaked. The painting was the important thing.

But he could not get off the sofa. And Heepish would not pay the slightest attention to his remarks about the painting. Neither would the guests.

He felt as if he were in a parallel universe which was in contact with that in Heepish's house but somewhat out of phase with it. He could communicate to a certain degree and then his words faded out. And, now that he looked around, this place seemed a trifle fuzzy.

Suddenly, he wondered if his coffee had been drugged.

It seemed so ridiculous that he tried to dismiss the thought. But if Heepish could steal his painting and hang it up where so many people would see it, knowing that word would quickly get to the man from whom he had stolen it, and if he could blandly, even friendlily, sit with the man from whom he had taken his property and act as if nothing were wrong, then such a man would have no compunction about drugging him.

But why would he want to drug him?

Thoughts of cellars with dirt floors and a six foot long, six foot deep trench in the dirt moved like a funeral train across his mind. A furnace in the basement burned flesh and bones. An acid pit ate away his body. He was roasted in an oven and this crew had him for dinner. He was immured, standing up, while Heepish and his guests toasted him with Amontillado. He was put in a cage in the basement and rats, scores of them, big hungry rats, were released into the cage. Afterwards, his clean-picked skeleton was wired together and stood up in this room as an extra macabre item. His friends and acquaintances, members of the Count Dracula Society and the Lord Ruthven League, would visit here because Heepish would become king after the great Forry Ackerman disappeared so mysteriously. They would see the skeleton and wonder whose it was – since so many people play Hamlet to the unknown Yoricks – and might even pat his bony head. They might even speak of Forry Ackerman in the presence of the skeleton.

Forry shook himself as a dog shakes himself emerging from water. He was getting a little psycho about this. All he had to do was to assert his rights. If Heepish objected, he would call the police. But he did not think that even Heepish would have the guts to stand in his way.

He stood up so suddenly he became even dizzier. He said, 'I'm taking my painting, Heepish! Don't get in my way!'

He turned around and stood up on the cushion and lifted the painting off its hook. There was a silence behind him, and when he turned, he saw that all were standing up, facing him. They formed a semicircle through which he would have to go to get to the door.

They looked grave, and their eyes seemed to have become larger and almost luminous. Almost, because it was his imagination that put a werewolfish gleam in them. Of course.

Mrs Pocyotl curled her lips back, and he saw that her canines were very long. How had he missed that feature when he first saw her? She had smiled, and it seemed to him that her teeth were very white and very even.

He stepped down off the sofa and said, 'I want my coat, Heepish.'

Heepish grinned. His teeth seemed to have become longer too. His gray eyes were as cold and hard as a winter sky in New York City.

'You may have your *coat*, Forry, since you don't want to be friendly.'

Forry understood the emphasis. Coat but not painting.

He said, 'I'll call the police.'

'You wouldn't want to do that,' Diana Rumbow said.

'Why not?' Forry said.

He wished his heart could beat faster. It should be, but it wasn't, even under this strain. Instead, his muscles were jerking, and his eyes were blinking twice as fast as usual, as if they were trying to substitute for the lack of heartbeats.

'Because,' the blonde said, 'I would accuse you of rape.'

'What?'

The painting almost slipped from his hands.

Diana Rumbow slipped out of her gown, revealing that she was wearing only a garter belt and nylon stockings. Her pubic hairs were long and very thick and a bright yellow. Her breasts, though large, did not sag.

Mrs Pocyotl said, 'Maybe you'd like two for the price of one, Forry.'

She slipped out of her gown, revealing that she wore only stockings and a belt. Her pubic hairs were black as a crow's feathers, and her breasts were conical.

Forry stepped back until the backs of his knees were in contact with the sofa. He said, 'What is this?'

'Well, *if* the police should be called, they would find this house deserted except for you and the two women. One woman would be unconscious and the other would be screaming. Both women would have sperm in their cunts, you can bet on that. And bruises. And you would be naked and dazed, as if you had, shall we say, gone mad with lust?'

Forry looked at them. All were grinning now, and they looked very evil. They also looked as if they meant to do whatever Heepish ordered.

He was in a nightmare. What kind of evil beings were these? All this for a painting?

He said, loudly. 'Get out of the way! I'm coming through! This painting is mine! And you're not going to intimidate me! I don't care what you do, you're not getting to keep this! I might have given it to you, Heepish, if you'd become a good friend and wanted it badly enough! But not now! So out of the way!'

Holding the painting as if it were a shield or a battering ram, he walked towards Heepish and the naked Rumbow.

# 7

Herald Childe drove slowly through the rain and the high waters. His windshield wipers were not able to cope at this moment, so dense was the downpour. His headlights strove to pierce the sheets with little effect. Other cars, driven by more foolhardy Angelenos, passed him with great splashings.

It took him more than two hours to get to his house in Topanga Canyon. He drove up the steep sidestreet at ten miles an hour while water, several inches deep, poured down past him. As he turned to go into his driveway, he noticed the car beneath the oak tree by the road. Another car that had been abandoned here, he supposed. There had been seven automobiles left here within the past several weeks. All were of the same model and year. All had been by the oak tree when he awoke in the morning. Some had been left for a week before the cops finally came and towed them away. Some had been there a few days and then had disappeared during the early morning hours.

He did not know why somebody was abandoning cars in front of his house or, if not outright abandoning them, was parking them for such a long time. His neighbors for two blocks on either side of the house and both sides of the street knew nothing about the cars.

The cops said that the cars they'd towed away were stolen.

So here was the seventh. Possibly the seventh. He must not jump to conclusions. It could belong to somebody visiting his neighbors. He would find out soon enough. Meanwhile, he needed to get to bed. To sleep. He had had more than enough of that other bedtime activity.

The house was his property. He owed nothing on it except the yearly taxes. It was a five room bungalow, Spanish style, with a big backyard and a number of trees. His aunt had willed it to him, and when she had died last year, he had moved in. He had not seen his aunt since 1942, when he had been a child, nor had he exchanged more than three letters with her in the past ten years. But she had left all her property to him. There was enough money so that he had the house left after using the money to pay off the inheritance tax.

Childe had been a private detective, but, after his experiences with Baron Igescu and the disappearance of his wife, he had quit. He wasn't a very good detective, he decided, and besides, he was sick of the business. He would go back to college, major in history, in which he had always been interested, get a master's and, possibly, a PhD in time. He would teach in a junior college at first and, later, in a university.

It would have been more convenient for him to take an apartment in Westwood where he would be close to the UCLA campus. But his money was limited, and he liked the house and the comparative quiet, so he drove every day to school. To save gas and also to find a parking place easier on the crowded campus, he rode a motorcycle during the week.

Just now the school was closed because of vacation.

It was a lonely life. He was busy studying because he was carrying a full load, and he had to keep up the house and the yard, but he still needed someone to talk to and to take to bed. There were women who came up to his house from time to time: teachers his own age or a little older, some older students, and, occasionally, a younger chick who dug his looks. He resembled a rough-hewn Lord Byron. *With a clubfoot mind*, he always added mentally when someone commented on this. It was no secret to him that he was neurotic. But then who wasn't? If that was any consolation.

He turned on the lights and checked the windows to make sure again that none were leaking. It was a compulsive action he went through before leaving and after coming back – at least three times each time. Then he looked out of the back window. The yard was narrow but deep, and this was good. Behind it towered a cliff of dirt, which had, so far, not become a mud flow. Water poured off it and drowned his backyard, and the water was up over the bottom steps of the back porch stairs. He understood from what his neighbors said, that the cliff had been closer to this house at one time. About ten years ago it had slid down and covered the backyard almost to the house. The aunt had spent much money having the dirt hauled away and a concrete and steel wire embankment built at the foot of the cliff. Then, two years ago, in the extraordinarily heavy rains, the cliff had collapsed again. It had, however, only buried the embankment and come about six feet into the yard. The aunt had done nothing about it, and, a year later, had died.

The entire Los Angeles, Ventura, and Orange County area was

43

being inundated. The governor was thinking about having Southern California declared a disaster area. Houses had floated away, mud slides had buried other houses, a car had disappeared in a hole in Ventura Boulevard, a woman waiting for a bus in downtown Los Angeles had been buried in a mud slide, houses were slipping in the Pacific Palisades and in the canyons everywhere.

There was only one consolation about the deluge. No smog.

Childe went into the kitchen and opened the pantry and took out a bottle of Jack Daniels. He seldom drank, preferring marijuana, but when he was downcast and upset, marijuana only made him more gloomy. He needed something to dull his mind and nerves, and Tennessee mash on the rocks would do it.

He sipped the stuff, shaking and making a face as he did so. After a while, he could swallow it without repugnance. A little later, he could sip on it with pleasure. He began to feel numb and even a trifle happy. The memory of Vivienne was still with him, but it did not shake him so much now.

The three men had entered and one had delicately placed the tip of his sword against Vivienne's neck. She had said something about his breaking the truce.

What truce? He had never found out. But the man with the sword cane had accused her and her people – he called them Ogs – of first breaking the truce. The Ogs had captured Childe and abused him. This was definitely against the rules. He was not even to be aware of their existence or of that of the Tocs.

Moreover, they had endangered Childe's life. He might have been killed because of their irresponsible behavior. In fact, the Tocs were not sure that the Ogs had not had it in mind to kill Childe.

'You know as well as you know anything that we agreed on The Face of Barrukh and the Testicle of Drammukh that we would let The Child develop until he was ready!' the swordsman said.

'The Child?' thought Herald. 'Or did he mean The Childe?'

Later, he thought, 'Possibly the two are the same.'

Vivienne, still crouching on the bed, had said, 'It was an accident that he came to our house – to Igescu's, I mean. He insisted on breaking in and spying on us, and the temptation to partake of his power was too much for us. In that, we were guilty. Then things got out of hand. We did not handle him correctly, I'll admit. We forgot that he would have to be watched very closely; he

44

looks so human it's easy to do, you know. And he acts so stupidly at times, he made us a little contemptuous of him.'

'Of The Child?' the swordsman said. 'I think you are the stupid ones. He is not an adult yet, you know, so you can't expect him to act like one. Anyway, I doubt the adulthood of any of you Ogs.'

Vivienne, looking then at Childe, said, 'We've been talking in English!'

She burst into a spew of a language which he had heard before even if it was unintelligible to him. It was the same language that his captors had used when he was a prisoner in Igescu's.

Though he did not understand what followed, he was able to determine the name of the swordsman. It was Hindarf.

Hindarf seemed inclined to run Vivienne through, but she talked him out of it. Finally, Hindarf pricked him with a needle, and presently he was able to function almost normally. He got dressed and allowed himself to be escorted out of the house. He was still too shaky to drive, so Hindarf drove while the other two men followed in their car. Hindarf refused to answer Childe's questions. His only comment was that Childe should stay away from the Ogs. Apparently, he had believed Vivienne's story that Childe was the intruder in this case.

A few blocks before they came to the turn-off to Topanga Canyon, Hindarf stopped the car. 'I think you can drive from here on.'

He got out and held the door open for a moment while the rain fell into the car and wet the driver's seat and the steering wheel.

He stuck his face into the car and said, 'Please don't go near that bunch again. They're deadly. You should know that. If it weren't . . .'

He was silent for several seconds and then said, 'Never mind. We'll be seeing you.'

He slammed the door shut. Childe scooted over into the driver's seat and watched Hindarf and the others drive away. Their car swung around and went down Topanga Canyon.

As he sat in the front room and tried to watch TV while he swigged Jack Daniels, he thought of that evening. Almost nothing made sense. But he did believe that Igescu and Krautschner and Bending Grass and Pao and the others had not been vampires, werewolves, werebears, or what have you. They were very strange, bordering on the unnatural or whatever humans thought of as unnatural. The theory advanced by Igescu, and presumably stated

45

by the early 19th-century Belgian, 'explained' the existence of these creatures. But Childe was beginning to think that Igescu had led him astray. He did not know why he would lie to him, but there seemed to be many things he did not know about this business.

If he had any sense, he would follow Hindarf's advice.

That was the trouble. He had never shown too much common sense.

*Fools rush in*, and so forth.

After four shots of mash whiskey on an empty stomach, one also unaccustomed to liquor, he went to bed. He slept uneasily and had a number of dreams and nightmares that he forgot as soon as he awoke.

The persistent ringing of the telephone woke him. He came up out of a sleep that seemed drugged, and was, if alcohol was a drug. He knocked the phone off while groping for it. When he picked it up, an unfamiliar male voice said, 'Is this McGivern's?'

'What number did you want?' Childe said.

The phone clicked. He looked at the luminous hands of his wristwatch. Three o'clock in the morning.

He tried to go back to sleep but couldn't. At ten after three, he got up and went into the bathroom for a drink of water. He did not turn on the light. Going out of the bathroom, he decided to check on the condition of the street before he went back to bed. It was still raining heavily, and the street had been ankle-deep in water when he had driven up before the house.

He pulled the curtain back and looked out. The car that had been parked under the oak tree was pulling away. The lights from the car behind it showed that a man was driving it. The car swung around and started slowly down the street towards Topanga Canyon. The lights of the other car shone on the pale face of Fred Pao, the Chinese he had seen at Igescu's. His lights threw the profiles of the three men in the other car into silhouette. One of them looked like Bending Grass, the Crow Indian, or Crow werebear, but that could not be. Bending Grass had died under the wheels of his car when Childe had escaped from the burning Igescu mansion.

He turned and ran into the bedroom and slipped into a pair of pants and shoes without socks. He ran into the front room, put on a rainhat and raincoat and picked up his wallet and car keys from the bowl of wax fruit – his aunt's legacy – on the dining room table. He got into the car and took off backwards, splashing water as if he were

46

surfriding as he backed on to the street. He drove faster than he should have and twice skidded and once the motor sputtered and he thought he had killed it.

He caught up with them about a quarter of a mile up Topanga. The lead car was slowing down even more and looked as if it would swing into a private road that went up the steep hill. He had never been up it, but he knew that it led to a huge three-storied house that had been built when the road was a dirt trail. It stood on top of a hill and overlooked much of the area, including his own house.

Abruptly, the lead car stopped. He had to go on by them; they would become suspicious if he also stopped. At the top of the hill he slowed down, found a driveway, turned in, and backed out. He came down the hill again in time to see the two cars heading back down Topanga Canyon.

He wondered what had made them change their minds? Had they become suspicious of him? Perhaps they had seen his lights as he turned on to Topanga?

Childe followed them into Los Angeles. The cars proceeded cautiously through the heavy rain and flooded streets until they reached San Vicente and La Cienega. When the light changed to green, the two cars suddenly roared into life. Shooting wings of water, their tires howling even on the wet pavement, they sped away. He accelerated after them. They swung left on reaching Sixth and skidded into the traffic island, bounced off, and continued back up San Vicente on the other side of the boulevard, then skidded right as they turned on Orange.

The green light was with them and with Childe, who was about a block behind. His rear tires hit the curb of the island and one wheel went over and there was a crash. He supposed his right fender had struck the traffic light, but it did not seem to impair the operation of the car. He shot after the other two cars, though he wondered why he was risking his limb and life. But the fact that they were trying so desperately to get away, that they had deliberately led him astray from that road up to the house on top of the hill, kept him going.

Nevertheless, when the car turned west on to Wilshire Boulevard, he began to think strongly about giving up the chase. They had gone through a red light without stopping and by the time he reached the intersection, he saw their taillights a block away. They were still casting out great sheafs of water.

He continued after them, increasing his speed. He did not know what he would do if he caught up with them. Four against one? And at least one of them, and probably all four, was a being with some very strange and deadly powers. He remembered Hindarf's words.

At Wilshire and San Vicente, the two cars went through a red light two seconds after it had changed. Two cars coming south on San Vicente met them. The lead car slammed broadside into Fred Pao's automobile, and the car behind the lead car smashed into its rear. The car following Pao rammed into his rear. A moment later, Childe's car, turning around and around on the wet pavement, slammed its rear into the car that had been following Pao's. The whole mass, five cars jammed into each other, swung around like a five-pointed star, around and around.

# 8

'Very well, Forry,' Heepish said. 'If you want it that badly . . .'

He bowed and made a flourish. Forry felt his cheeks warming up. He said, 'Do I *want* it? It's *mine*! I paid for it with my money! You stole it, like a common thief!'

'No common thief would touch it,' Heepish said.

Forry, deciding that absolutely nothing was to be gained by standing there, plunged on ahead. The others opened a way for him, and Heepish even ran up and opened the door for him.

'See you, Forry,' he said.

'Yeah. In jail, maybe!'

As soon as he was in his own house, Forry placed the painting on the wall and then checked the doors to make sure they were locked. The Dummocks had not come home yet, so he decided to stay and sleep on the couch that night. Then he remembered that he was supposed to get the latest edition of *Vampirella* out. He had completely forgotten about it!

He made himself some coffee and went into a rear room, where his 'office' was. He worked away steadily until 2:30, when he heard a slight noise somewhere in the house. He rose and started out of the office when the lights went out. That was all he needed to put him hopelessly behind schedule!

He fumbled around in the desk drawer for matches which he did not think he would have, since he had never smoked. Finding none, he groped through to the kitchen. The pantry shelves were filled with books and magazines. He did not eat at the house but took all his meals out or ate at Wendy's. The icebox, except for some cream for coffee and a few goodies, was filled with microfilm.

As he felt around in the porch room for a flashlight, the lights suddenly came back on. He continued until he found the flashlight. If the power failed again, he would work by its light.

On the way back to the office, he looked into the front room. The Stoker painting was gone!

There was no time to stand around and think. He put on his

rainhat and raincoat and rubbers and walked as fast as his heart would let him out to the car. He got into the big green Cadillac and backed out into the lake which Sherbourne Drive had become. He went as fast as he dared and within two minutes was before Woolston Heepish's. Fred Pao, the painting in his arms, was just turning away from the car.

Forry blasted his horn at him and flicked his brights on. The Chinese was startled and almost dropped the painting. Forry cried out in anguish and then lowered the window to shout at Pao.

'I'll call the police!'

Pao opened the rear door of the car and shoved the painting into it. He ran around to the other side, got in, and the motor roared. His Mercury took off with a screeching of tires and sped towards Olympic. Forry stared at him for several seconds and then, biting his lip, took off with a similar screeching of tires. At the same time, he honked furiously at the Chinese. The man was taking his beloved Dracula where he could hide it until the search was up. And then Woolston Heepish would receive it!

But not if Forest J Ackerman, the Gray Lensman of Los Angeles, had anything to do with it! Just as Buck Rogers trailed Killer Kane to his lair, so FJA would track down the thief!

Pao's car swung west on Olympic. Forry started to go through the stop sign, too, but had to slam on his brakes as a car going west on Olympic, sheets of water flying from its sides, honked at him. His car skidded and slid sidewise out on to the main boulevard. The oncoming car swerved and skidded also, turned around once, and ended up still going westward. Forry straightened out the Cadillac and ran it as if it were a speedboat. Waves curling out on both sides, he passed the car he had almost hit and then continued building up speed until he saw Pao's taillights going right on Robertson. He went through a red light, causing two cars to apply their brakes and honk their horns. He chased Pao up Robertson and down Charleville Boulevard. Despite its multiplicity of stop signs, neither stopped once. Then Pao turned up to Wilshire, went westward back to Robertson, up Robertson, through all intersections with stop signs and signal lights red or green, and skidded right on Burton Way. He ran a red light going to San Vicente and so did Forry. In the distance a police siren whooped, and Forry almost slowed down. But he decided that he could justify his speeding and, even if he couldn't, a fine would be worth it if the cops caught Pao with the stolen goods. He hoped the cops would show up in time. If they didn't, they might find one dead Chinese.

Pao continued down San Vicente, ran another red light at Sixth, with Forry two car-lengths behind him. Despite their recklessness, neither was going over forty. The water was too solid; at higher speeds it struck the bottom of the car like a club.

At Wilshire and San Vicente the light was green for them, but two cars raced through the red, and Pao hit the lead car broadside. Forry applied his brakes and slowed down the car somewhat, but it crashed into the rear of the Chinese's car. His head hit something, and he blacked out.

# 9

Childe was half-dazed. After the screaming of rubber, the crashing and ripping and rending of metal, and the shatter and tinkle of glass, there was a moment of silence – except for the rain and a siren in the distance. Some of the cars still had operating headlights, and these cast a pale rain-streaked halo over the wreckage. Then a huge black fox leaped on to the top of his hood, paused to grin through the windshield at him, leaped down on to the street, and trotted off into the darkness behind Stats Restaurant.

The police car, its siren dying, pulled up by the cars, and two officers got out. At the same time, a big dog – no, a wolf – passed by him, also on the way to the rear of the restaurant.

An officer, looking into the cars, swore and called to his partner. 'Hey, Jeff, look at this! Two piles of clothes in this one and another pile in this car and nobody around that could have worn them! What the hell is this?'

The policeman had a genuine mess in more ways than one. No one seemed to be dead or even seriously hurt. Childe's car was bashed in in the front and side but was still operable. The car of a Mr Ackerman had a smashed radiator and would have to be towed away. Pao's car was destroyed. The others were leaking badly from the radiators and could not be driven far.

One policeman set out flares. The other still could not get over the abandoned clothing. He kept muttering, 'I've seen some freak things, but this tops them all.'

Another patrol car arrived after fifteen minutes. The officers determined that no one needed to be hospitalized. They took down the necessary information, gave out some tickets, and then dismissed the participants. The case was far from over, but there had been so many accidents because of the rain and so many other duties to perform that the police had to streamline normal procedures. One did say that the two Mr Paos and Mr Batlang would be sought for leaving the scene of an accident. And if the clothes meant anything, they might be arrested for public nudity, indecent exposure and, probably, would be subjected to a psychiatric examination.

One of the passengers in the car said that they must have been dazed. He knew them well, they were responsible citizens, and they would never leave the scene of an accident unless they had been rendered half-conscious in a state of shock.

'Maybe so,' the policeman said. 'But you have to admit it's rather peculiar that all three should take off their clothes – slide out of them the way it looks to me – and run away. We were right behind you, and we didn't even see them leave.'

'It was raining very heavily,' the passenger said.

'Not that heavily.'

'What a night,' the other policeman said.

Childe tried to talk to the others in the accident, but only Forrest J (no period) Ackerman would reply. He seemed very concerned about a painting in the rear of Pao's car. He had removed it shortly after the police had arrived and put it in the back seat of his Cadillac. If the police observed this, they did not say anything. Now he wanted to get it back to his house.

'I'll take you as soon as they let us go,' Childe said. 'Your house isn't far from here; it won't be any bother.'

He did not know what Ackerman's part in this was. He seemed to be an innocent victim, but then there was the transfer of the painting from Pao's car. How had Pao gotten hold of it? Also, there seemed to be two Paos. Were they twins?

Forry Ackerman told him something of what had happened on the way to his house. Childe became very excited, because he had met Woolston Heepish when he was investigating the disappearance of his partner, Colben. Another friend had taken him to Heepish's because Heepish had a large file on 'vampire' cases, and the film sent to the LAPD showed a Dracula-type vampire assisting in the mutilation of Colben.

Childe decided that he would appear to go along with Ackerman's story. The man seemed to be sincere and genuinely upset and puzzled by what had happened. But it was possible that he was one of the Ogs, as Hindarf called them. It was also possible that he was one of the Tocs.

When he drove up before Ackerman's house, he looked at it through the dark and the rain, and he said, 'If I didn't know better, I would think Heepish lived here.'

'That man deliberately fixed his house to look like mine,' Forry said. 'That's why he's called the poor man's Forry Ackerman, though I don't think he's so poor.'

They went inside and, while Ackerman hung the painting, Childe looked around. The layout of the house was the same, but the paintings and the other items were different. And this place was brighter and more inclined to science-fiction subjects than Heepish's.

When Forry stepped down off the sofa with a satisfied smile, Childe said, 'There's something wrong about this accident, other than the disappearance of Pao. I mean, I was chasing Pao in one car and the three men with him in the other. Yet you say you were chasing Pao, too.'

'That's right,' Forry said. 'It is puzzling. The whole evening has been puzzling and extremely upsetting. I have to get the latest issue of my comic book out to my publisher in New York, and I'm far behind. I'll have to work twice as fast to catch up.'

Childe interpreted this as meaning that he should leave at once. The man must really be dedicated to his work. How many could go back to their desk and work on a piece of fiction about vampires when they might have been associating with genuine vampires, not to mention genuine werefoxes and werewolves?

'When you get your work done, and you're ready to talk,' Childe said, 'we'll get together. I have many questions, and I also have some information you might find interesting, though I don't know that you'll believe it.'

'I'm too tired to believe in anything but a good night's sleep, which I'm not going to get,' Forry said. 'I hate to be inhospitable, but . . .'

Childe hesitated. Should he take up more of this man's time by warning him? He decided that it would be better not to. If he knew what danger he was really in, he would not be able to concentrate on his work. And knowing the danger would not help him in the least unless he believed in it and fled from this area. That did not seem likely. Childe would not have believed such a story if he had not experienced it.

He gave Forry his phone number and address and said, 'Call me when you're ready to talk this over. I have a lot to tell you. Maybe, together, we can get a more complete picture.'

Forry said he would do so. He conducted Childe to the door but before he let him through, he said, 'I think I'll take that painting into my office with me. I wouldn't put it past Heepish to try again.'

Childe did not ask why he did not call the police. Obviously, if he did, he would be held up even more in getting out *Vampirella*.

# 10

Herald Childe did not get home until seven in the morning. The rain had stopped by four thirty, but the canyons were roaring streams. He was stopped by the police, but when he explained that he lived off the main road, he was permitted to go on. Only residents could use this section of Topanga Canyon, and they were warned that it would be better if they stayed away. Childe pushed on – literally – and eventually got to his driveway. He saw three houses that had slipped their moorings and moved downhill anywhere from six to twenty feet. Two of the houses must have been deserted, but outside the third a family was moving some furniture and clothes into the back of a pickup truck. Childe thought momentarily about helping them and then decided that they could handle their own affairs. The pickup truck was certainly more equipped to move through the high water than his low-slung car, and if they wanted to break their backs moving their sofa, that was their foolish decision.

Another car of the same year and model as the others was parked under the branches of the oak tree. The water flowing down the street was up past the hubs of the wheels. So strong was the force of the current, it sometimes lifted Childe's car a fraction of an inch. But at no time was it more than one wheel off the ground.

He parked the car in the driveway. The garage floor was flooded and, besides, he wanted the car available for a quick takeoff. He was not sure that the water pouring off the cliff and drowning his backyard would not lift the garage eventually. Or, if the cliff did collapse, it might move far enough to smash the garage, which was closer to the cliff than the house.

He unlocked the door and locked it behind him. He started to cross the room when, in the pale daylight, a shapeless form rose from the sofa. He thought his heart would stop.

The shapelessness fell off the figure. It was a blanket which had disguised it.

For a moment, he could not grasp who was standing before him. Then he cried, 'Sybil!'

It was his ex-wife.

She ran to him and threw her arms around him, put her face against his chest, and sobbed. He held her and whispered, over and over, 'Sybil! Sybil! I thought you were dead! My God, where have you been?'

After a while she quit crying and raised her face to kiss him. She was thirty-four now, her birthday had been six days ago, but she looked as if she had aged five years. There were large dark circles under her eyes and the lines from nose to mouth had gotten deeper. She also seemed thinner.

He led her to the sofa and sat her down and then said, 'Are you all right?'

She started to cry again, but after a minute she looked up at him and said, 'I am and I'm not.'

'Is there anything I can do for you?' he asked.

'Yes, you can give me a cup of coffee. And a joint, if you have one.'

He waved his hand as if to indicate a complete change of character. 'I don't have any pot. I've gone back to drinking.'

She looked alarmed, and he said, hastily, 'Only a shot very infrequently. I'm going to school again. UCLA. History major.'

Then, 'How did you find this house? How did you get here? Is that your car out in front?'

'I was brought up here by somebody – somebodies – and let into the house. I took off the blindfold and looked around. I found my photograph on your bedside table, so I knew where I was. I decided to wait for you, and I fell asleep.'

'Just a minute,' he said. 'This is going to be a long story, I can see that. I'll make some coffee and some sandwiches, too, in case we get hungry.'

He did not like to put off hearing what had happened, but he knew that he would not want to be interrupted after she got started. He did everything that had to be done very swiftly and brought in a tray with a big pot of coffee, food, and some rather dried-out cigarettes he found in the pantry. He no longer smoked, but he had gotten cigarettes for women he had brought into the house.

Sybil said, 'Oh, good!' and reached for the cigarettes. Then she withdrew her hand and said, wearily, 'I haven't smoked for six months, and my lungs feel much better. I won't start up again.'

She had said this before and sounded as if she meant it. But this time her voice had a thread of steel in it. Something had happened to change her.

57

'All right,' he said. 'You left for your mother's funeral in San Francisco. I called your sister, and she said you'd phoned her and told her you couldn't get a plane out and your car wouldn't start. You told her you were coming up with a friend, but you hung up without saying who the friend was. And that was the last I heard of you. Now, over a year later, you show up in my house.'

She took a deep breath and said, 'I don't expect you to believe this, Herald.'

'I'll believe anything. With good reason.'

'I couldn't get hold of you, and, anyway, after that horrible quarrel, I didn't think you'd want to ever see me again. I had to get to San Francisco, but I didn't know how. Then I thought of a friend of mine, and I walked over to his apartment. He only lived a block from me.'

'He?'

'Bob Guilder. You don't know him.'

'A lover?' he said, feeling a pinprick of jealousy. Thank God that emotion was dying out, in regard to her, anyway.

'Yes,' she said. 'Earlier. We parted but not because we couldn't stand one another. We just didn't strike fire off each other, sexually. But we remained fairly good friends. Anyway, I got there just as he was packing to leave for Carmel. He couldn't stand the smog anymore, and even though the governor didn't want people leaving, he said he was going anyway. He was glad to drive me all the way into San Francisco, since he had some things to do there.'

They had driven out Ventura Boulevard because the San Diego Freeway was jammed, according to the radio. At a standstill. Ventura Boulevard was not much better, but ten miles an hour was an improvement over no miles.

Just off the Tarzana ramp, the car over-heated. Guilder managed to get it into Tarzana, but there was only one service station operating. The proprietors of the others were either staying home or were also attempting to get out of the deadly smog.

'You won't believe this,' she said, 'but I stole a motorcycle. It was sitting by the curb, its key in the ignition. There was no one in sight, although the owner may have been only thirty feet away, the smog was that thick. I've ridden Hondas before, did you know that? Another friend of mine used to take me out on one for fun, and he taught me how to ride it.'

And other things, thought Childe without pain. The thought was automatic, but he was glad that it did not mean much now.

There had been no use in her trying to reach 'Frisco on the Honda. The traffic was so thick and slow-moving that she did not see any chance of getting to her destination until the funeral was over, if then. She decided to return to her apartment. Eyes burning, sinuses on fire, lungs hurting, she rode the Honda home. That took two hours. The cars were filling both sides of the street, all going in the same direction, but there was enough room, if she took the sidewalk now and then, to travel.

She got to her apartment, and five minutes afterwards, someone knocked on her door. She thought it must be another tenant. Without a key, it was difficult to get into the building.

But she did not recognize the two men, and before she could shut the door, they were on her. She felt a needle enter her arm, and she became unconscious. When she awoke, she was in a suite of three rooms, not including the bathroom. All were large and luxuriously furnished, and throughout her captivity she was given the best of food and liquor, cigarettes and marijuana, and anything she desired for her body.

Except clothes. She had one beautiful robe and two flimsy negligees which were cleaned each week.

When she awoke, she was alone. She prowled around and found that there were no windows and the two doors were locked. There was a big color TV set and a radio, both of which worked. The telephone was not connected to the outside line. When she lifted it, she heard a man's voice answer, and she put the receiver down without saying anything. A few minutes later, a door swung open, and two men and a woman came in.

She described them in detail when Childe asked how they looked. One of them could be one of the Paos; the woman had to be Vivienne Mabcrough. The second man did not sound like anyone he knew.

Sybil became hysterical, and they injected her once more. When she woke up again, she controlled herself. She was told that she would not be harmed and that, eventually, she would be released. When she asked them what they wanted her for, she got no answers. Over the year's time, she concluded that her captors were planning on using her, somehow, as a weapon or lever against Childe.

Childe, thinking of the sexual abuse he had suffered during his short imprisonment in the Igescu house, could not conceive that she was not molested in any way. He asked her if she had been raped.

59

'Oh, many times!' she said, almost matter-of-factly.

'Did they hurt you?' She did not seem to be affected by his question or any painful memories.

'A little bit, at first,' she said.

'How do you feel now? I mean, were the experiences psychologically traumatic?'

He was beginning to feel like a psychiatrist or, perhaps, a prosecuting attorney.

'Come here, sit down by me,' she said. She held out a slim and pale hand. He came to her and put his arm around her and kissed her. He expected her to burst into tears again, but she only sighed. After a while, she said, 'I've always been very frank with you, right?'

'Yes. But I don't know that a compulsion to honesty was the main factor,' he said. 'That may have been your rationalization, but I thought that your frankness was more to hurt me than anything else.'

'You might be right,' she said. She sipped on some coffee and then said, 'I'll tell you what happened to me, but it won't be to hurt you. I don't think so, anyway.'

# 11

Sybil exercised, smoked more than was good for her, watched TV and listened to radio, read the magazines and books supplied whenever she asked for them, and generally tried to keep from going crazy. The uncertainty of her position was the largest element pushing her towards insanity. However, it was not as bad as being in solitary. The man who answered the phone would talk to her, and she got visitors at least five times a day. The woman who brought her meals would sit with her and talk when asked to do so, and a man called Plugger and a woman called Panchita came quite often. Occasionally, the fantastically beautiful Vivienne Mabcrough would drop in.

'They talked to me about many things, but they also asked many questions about you,' Sybil said. 'Mostly what I knew about your childhood, although they also wanted to know about your personal habits, what you read, your dreams – imagine that, your dreams! – and other things I might just happen to know because I was your wife.'

Sybil had seen nothing damaging to Herald in this. Besides, her drive to honesty almost forced her to give them complete answers. Or that was her rationalization.

After a while, she began to suffer from sexual deprivation. Her nipples swelled whenever they touched cloth. Her cunt itched. She found herself sitting with her foot under her and rocking back and forth on the heel or rubbing up against the bed post or the back of a chair. She even kept a banana from her meal and masturbated with it.

'If it's any consolation to you,' she said, 'I fantasized that you were my lover. Mostly, that is.'

He did not ask her who the others were. Actually, he did not care anymore. And that was strange, because he was feeling a genuine warmth and affection for her, perhaps even a love. He was happy to see her again and to be with her.

Sybil may have changed but she had not changed completely. She still had to tell him everything.

'You needn't be jealous of the other man,' she said. 'He doesn't exist. He's a fiction. Can you guess who?'

'This isn't exactly the time for guessing games,' he said. 'But no, I don't know who you imagined at the other end of the banana.'

'Tarzan!' she said.

'Tarzan? Oh, for cripe's sake! Well, why not? Bananas, big dongs, and all that. It only stands to reason that the superman of the jungle would be hung heavy.'

He was sarcastic, but he was also surprised. There were still things about her he did not know. Tarzan!

There might have been a closed circuit TV monitoring her, she said. Otherwise, why would Plugger enter that evening, and tell her she did not need to suffer anymore?

Plugger was a tall, rangy man with a deep tan, black hair which came down in a widow's peak, somewhat pointed ears, and a very handsome face. He stood before her and stripped while she asked him what he thought he was doing, though she knew well enough.

'He had a beautiful body with the smoothest skin, almost like glass. But his cock was big. Not enormous, just big and thick and it had the biggest knob at the end of it I've ever seen. I don't mean the glans. That was big enough, but he had a growth, I guess you could call it a wart, on the side of the head. I told him that really turned me off.'

'You sound as if you were pretty cool about the whole thing,' he said.

'Well, I was suffering. The banana was a long way off from being perfectly satisfactory. Or perfectly satisfying. And he was a hell of a good-looking man, and he talked with me enough so that I rather liked him, even if he was my warder. So I just told myself, you know, the cliché, if you have to be raped, lean back and enjoy it.'

'Really?' he said.

'Well, not really. I was scared. But then he said he wouldn't force me. That helped relax me a lot.'

Plugger sat down by her and kissed her. She tried to turn her head away, but he turned it gently back. She protested that he was forcing her, and he replied that he only asked for one kiss. If she did not like it, he would not kiss her again.

That seemed fair to her, really more than she had expected. After all, if he wanted to rape her, he could.

She lifted her face to him at the same time that he put her hand on his cock and his tongue into her mouth.

The shock that went down her throat and up her arm was almost as if she had touched an electric eel.

'I mean, it was something like an electrical shock but much weaker. I had an orgasm in my throat and up my arm.'

Childe jumped up and said, 'What?'

'Yes, I know. It sounds crazy. But it was true. I came. I mean, you know, when I come, I come with my whole body. But the ecstasy was denser, I mean, more intense, in my mouth and throat and in my hand and arm.'

He did not say anything more. His experiences with Igescu's crew had opened doors to an exotic enough world. Plugger was one that he had not experienced, and he supposed that there were many other outré beings in that group.

Sybil had not resisted when he took her robe and negligee off. She had allowed him to move her on to the bed, where he got between her legs and thrust his tongue into her cunt. It was like a spark in a cylinder full of vaporized gas. Orgasm after orgasm exploded in her, and then they began building up more slowly, building until she could endure the exquisiteness no more and felt that she would faint.

While she lay panting and moaning with the aftermath, he climbed on to her and pressed her breasts around his dong. The same shock passed through them; the ecstasy was so intense she could see – but of course it was imagination – blue sparks sputtering from the tips of her nipples.

'The funny thing was, his prick was soft,' she said. 'Even when he stuck it into my mouth, and transmitted that electrical come, it stayed soft.'

'He didn't come in your mouth?' he said. 'I mean, spermatic fluid?'

'There wasn't any gism, no. I mean, that shock, you might say, was a sort of electrical come.'

She had gone into a series of orgasms, one after the other, so fast that she could not count them.

After this, he kissed her all over, and every inch of her skin felt a minor orgasm until he stuck his tongue up her anus. That almost lifted her off the bed, and she did faint after that orgasm.

She was silent then, as if dwelling with great pleasure on the memory.

Childe finally spoke. 'Well, did he ever stick his prick in your cunt?'

He had not meant to sound so harsh but, for the first time, he was jealous.

'No. I tried to get it in even after he said it was no use. It kept doubling back and falling out. But I got orgasms through my hand while I was trying to do it. I said I was sorry I couldn't do something for him. He said it did not matter; he was more than satisfied. I guess that I wasn't far wrong when I said his come was electrical. He had a high-voltage gism, you might say.'

She had questioned him about this phenomenon, which became frightening when she recovered enough to think about it. He replied that he was built differently, and he got up, picked up his clothes, and walked out.

He came every four days after that. She asked him why he did not visit her more often, and he said it took time for him to build up a charge. She took him literally, but she was beginning to get frightened again. What kind of weirdos were these? However, when he touched her, her fright went away.

After about five visits from Plugger, two women, Panchita and Diana, came to her room. They talked for a while and left. Every few days, they would drop in. Then, one afternoon, Panchita asked her if she would like some pot. Sybil was very eager to get some, because it would help to pass away the dull moments of her existence. All three lit up.

'But it wasn't real pot,' she said. 'It smelled something like pot, but it must have been something else. It really turned me on, but it also made me very suggestible. I think it had some hypnotic element in it.'

'Really?' Childe said. He anticipated what she was going to relate.

'Yes. I got pretty high, and all three of us were laughing hysterically. I had completely forgotten that I was their prisoner and at their mercy. They seemed like very old friends and very lovable. In fact, uh, desirable.'

'One of them made love to you?'

'Oh, yes. Panchita sat down by me and quite casually put her arm around my shoulder. The next I knew, she was cupping my breast with her other hand and then stroking my nipple. I felt a great deal of love – and lust – for Panchita. It seemed the most natural thing in the world. You know I don't swing that way, Herald. I have never had a homosexual experience in my life, not until then. In fact, the idea used to make me sick.'

64

Childe said nothing.

She continued: 'Diana, the tall blonde with perfectly enormous breasts, sat down on my other side. She started to kiss me while Panchita pulled up my negligee and began to suck on my nipple. I felt as if I was on fire. I tongued Diana's mouth while she tongued mine. And then I felt Panchita's mouth going down my belly. She kissed me all over there but stopped when she came to my cunt.

'Diana lifted me up then and walked me over to the bed, where she took off my negligee. I got on to the bed and on my back and Diana and Panchita took their clothes off. They stood on each side of the bed and each took one of my hands and placed it against her cunt. They were dripping with lubricating fluid, sopping. I stuck a finger in each slit, and they moved their hips back and forth and jacked themselves off.'

'Is it necessary to go into such detail?' Childe said.

'It's good therapy for me,' she said. Her eyes were closed, and her head was leaning against the back of the sofa.

The two women had climbed in beside her. Diana kissed and fondled her breasts while Sybil caressed Diana's left breast. Panchita again traveled down her belly with the tip of her tongue. After tracing a triangle around the pubic hairs with her tongue, Panchita got down between Sybil's legs. She spread them apart and then slid a pillow under her buttocks. The next Sybil knew, Panchita was running her tongue over her clitoris and sticking it up her cunt as far as she could. She kept at it until Sybil had an orgasm.

'Then Panchita traded places with Diana, and Diana tongue-fucked me,' she said. 'Diana stimulated me better, I came about five times. Then Panchita got on top of me, and I licked her cunt and put my tongue up her slit and vibrated its tip against her clitoris. She came a number of times, after which Diana got on top of me. Diana came almost at once.

'Then Panchita got down again and turned me on my side and licked my asshole while Diana licked my cunt again. When I had come a number of times, we made a triangle, mouth to pussy, you might say, fingers up twats, and, and, it was wonderful!'

'You say that even in retrospect?'

'I didn't that night after they left. I cried, and I felt so disgusted and dirty. The drug had worn off by then, you understand. But Panchita and Diana kept visiting me, and after a while, I quit having guilty feelings. I got to liking it. Why not? What's so bad about making love to women? Does it hurt anyone?'

'No,' he said. 'Did their lovemaking lessen the effect of Plugger's?'

'Not at all. Actually, if you were to rate orgasms on a scale, I'd have to rate him as Super A-Plus and theirs as B-Minus.'

'Next you'll be telling me that Plugger and the two women got into bed with you at the same time,' he said.

She opened her eyes and turned her head to look at him.

'How'd you know that?' she said. 'Pour me another cup of coffee, will you, honey?'

He passed her the full cup and said, 'Did Plugger touch off the two women, too?'

'Oh, yes. Once Panchita and Diana and I got down in a daisy chain, and he rammed his tongue up Panchita's ass. He said she had the sweetest asshole, which made me a little jealous. Would you believe it, all three of us felt the shock in our cunts and our mouths? That electricity or whatever it was passed through all of us.'

'I can understand your making love to the women the first time,' he said. 'You were under the influence of that drug you smoked. But you knew how it affected you, so why didn't you refuse to smoke it the next time they offered it to you?'

'Like I said, I enjoyed it. Anyway, I didn't think about refusing it the second time. I don't know why.'

'Your mind shut down,' he said. 'You wanted to go to bed with them, so you just forgot how the stuff would affect you.'

'I'm not a compulsive Lesbian!' she cried. 'I don't have any neurotic drive for women! I can take them or leave them!'

'You just got out of prison, so how would you know?' he said. 'However, that doesn't matter. Not now, anyway. How did they explain giving you a hypnotic drug when they said they wouldn't force you?'

'They explained that they did not force me to smoke the pot, or what they called pot. And, later, they said I didn't have to smoke it now that I knew the effects.'

'You aren't hooked on the stuff?'

'Absolutely not!'

'Well, you may be right. Time will tell. I just don't understand their nonsadistic treatment. If you hadn't described certain people that I know so well, I would say that another group besides Igescu's had you.'

'What are you talking about? Another group?'

'I'll tell you later about my adventures, if you can call them that.'

She continued with her story. He wondered if it was just that: a story. There was no doubt that she knew Panchita Pocyotl and Diana Rumbow and others and to do so she must have been held prisoner. But this sexual narrative? Had it really happened the way she said, or was she unconsciously concealing something more terrible. Had she suffered such traumatic handling that she was repressing it and substituting a fantasy? It did not seem likely, because she did not act psychotic, but then a psychotic often acted normally.

If the Ogs, as Hindarf called them, had treated her relatively considerately, then they had some sinister end in mind.

There was one confirmation of her story, he thought. That was that Vivienne Mabcrough had left her alone.

'And then, one afternoon, this fabulously beautiful woman, Vivienne, came to my room,' she said.

'Oh?'

Vivienne and Sybil smoked the marijuana-like substance, with Sybil knowing well what was coming. The two made love, but the snake thing remained within Vivienne's womb. Sybil was not aware of its existence, and Childe did not mention it.

Vivienne came to Sybil many times after that, sometimes alone and sometimes with Panchita or Diana or Plugger or with all three. Then Fred Pao, or his twin, showed up. Both only wanted to be sucked off, but when Sybil refused unless she was given something in return, they brought Plugger in with them. While Sybil stood in the middle of the room, bent over, sucking on Pao's long slim dick, Plugger pressed his electric cock against her anus or held its tip against her cunt. Sometimes, he got down on his knees and spread the cheeks of her ass and rammed his tongue up it.

'Every prisoner should have it so good,' Childe said. He was thinking of what had happened to Colben and the others and what might have happened to him. But, now that he considered it, Igescu's group may not have been planning mutilation and death for him. They seemed to have been aware that he was something special, if he could believe what Hindarf and Vivienne had said in their short conversation in English.

However, they had been trying to kill him after he had escaped and killed some of them. This could have been from self-defense only, not from a desire to murder for the pleasure of murder.

Mysteriouser and mysteriouser, he thought, paraphrasing Alice.

And Sybil had been a sort of Alice in Sexland. Certainly her adventures were as strange as Alice's.

'You never found anything peculiar about Vivienne?' he said.

'No. Should I have?'

This seemed to confirm her story about her gentle treatment. If Vivienne had revealed the snake-thing, and the two had made love to Sybil, then she was being very considerate of Sybil.

Despite all this enjoyment and the use of drugs, Sybil had many periods of depression, frustration, and a desire to get away. There were times when she felt as if she were a cow being fattened up for slaughter. And even after she became quite at ease with her captors and talked fluently, she could not get them to answer one question about the reason for her imprisonment.

And then, two days ago, all her visitors, except for a woman who brought her meals now and then, quit coming. The woman would not even say Good Morning to her, let alone answer questions. Sybil had watched TV and smoked pot and wondered what was going on. Her fears came to the surface, and she fantasized many dreadful things happening to her.

Then, this very night, she was awakened by a hand shaking her. She sat up in bed, her heart throbbing painfully, to find three masked men by her bedside. One told her to get dressed. She did so, while they packed for her. They had brought her clothes in from someplace, presumably from a closet in the house. Then they blindfolded her and took her out of the house and drove her here. The drive, she estimated, had lasted two hours.

Childe did not say anything, but it seemed to him that she could have been located much closer than two hours' drive to his house. If she were prisoner in that house near his, her rescuers might have driven around to make it seem that she had been a long ways from him.

On the other hand, she might have been held in, say, Vivienne's house in Beverly Hills.

'Do you feel all right?' he said.

'What? Oh, yes, I feel fine, except for being tired. And I am happy that I'm out of that, although it wasn't an altogether unpleasurable experience. But very puzzling. What do you think made Plugger th way he was? I mean, how about that electricity of his? Do you think he had a surgically implanted battery of some sort? It sounds sort of science-fiction, doesn't it?'

He kissed her and said, 'What about some nice normal sex?'

'All right,' she murmured. 'It's late and I'm tired, but I would like to have a man who's really in love with me. You are in love with me, aren't you? Despite all our troubles?'

'I must be,' he said. 'There have been times this past year when I was almost out of my mind wondering what could have happened to you.'

He stood up and said, 'I'll get into my pajamas after I shower and shave.'

'I'm clean,' she said. 'I'll wait right here for you. You can carry me to bed. It'll be so nice.'

Ten minutes later, having sped through his preparations, he returned to the front room. She was sitting slumped on the sofa, fast asleep. He grinned wryly and kissed her on the forehead, moved her so that she was stretched out on the sofa, put the blanket over her, kissed her forehead again, and went into his bedroom. The rain had started again.

# 12

Forrest J Ackerman awoke with his head on the desk and the finally edited package of the latest issue of *Vampirella* beside him. He got up and shook his head. When he had finished his work this morning, he had intended to rush down to the post office on Robertson and mail it out. But he had somehow fallen asleep.

The first thought was: The painting! Had he been drugged so that it could be stolen again?

But it was leaning against the wall by the desk. He sighed with relief, part of which could be repressed anger at Woolston Heepish. Something really should be done about that fellow. He was not only a thief, he was dangerous. Anybody who would get two women to strip in order to seduce him out of the painting – and before witnesses – was not only dangerous, he was mad.

Forry stumbled into the kitchen, washed his face in the sink, and then picked up the bulky envelope containing *Vampirella*. He was outside before he remembered that he did not have a car. One more count against Woolston Heepish!

At that moment, like the Gray Lensman or Batman arriving to save the situation, the Dummocks drove up. Lorenzo crawled out of the car and, on all fours, progressed slowly towards the house. He was a youth of thirty-five, of medium height, black haired, ruddy faced, black moustached, paunched, and skinny legged. Hulia, his wife, could walk, but just barely. She was a short woman with a magnificent bust, a hawk face, dark hair, and thick spectacles. She was thirty.

Forry said, 'I'd like to borrow your car. I have to run to the post office.'

'All yours,' said Lorenzo, not looking up at him.

'The keys,' Forry said. 'The keys.'

'You want Hulia, you can have her. The cunt's all yours. Just keep me in cigarettes, food, booze, and typing paper, and she's all yours, Forry, old buddy. Ask her, she doesn't mind.'

'I want the keys to your car, not your wife!' Forry said loudly.

Lorenzo continued to crawl towards the door. He turned his head and said, 'Hulia! Hurry up, help me up! Got the keys?'

Hulia stood swaying and blinking, looking like a giant drunken owl. 'What keys? To the car or the house?'

'Fuck it! Forry, can you open the door for me?'

Forry looked into the car. As he had suspected the keys were still in the ignition. He did not see how Lorenzo could have driven in his condition without smashing up, but the luck of drunkards and egoists had held out.

He walked back and opened the door for the two. After Lorenzo had crawled in and Hulia had fallen on her face crossing the threshold, he started to close the door. But he said, 'Don't you dare puke on any of my stuff! You do, and out you go! Pronto!'

'Why, Forry!' Hulia said. 'Have we ever puked on anything of yours?'

'Just my creature from the Black Lagoon bust,' Forry said. 'I forgave you, since it could be cleaned. But if you vomit on any of my books or paintings, or anything at all anymore, out you go!'

'You must really be mad at us, Forry darling!' Hulia said. 'I've never seen you angry before. I thought you were a saint!'

'If I puke, you can have Hulia,' Lorenzo said, looking up from his supine position in the middle of the floor. 'Just so you don't toss our ass out of here. I'm writing the Great Cosmic Novel now, Forry. Not the Great American Novel. The Cosmic Novel. It makes Tolstoy, Dostoyevsky, and Norman Mailer look sick. I'm really the greatest creator of them all, Forry, my Maecenas, patron of the arts, protector of the gifted and genius. Your name will go down in history as Forrest J (No Period) Ackerman, the man who gave Lorenzo Dummock a roof over his head, a bed to sleep in, a desk to write on, food, booze, cigarettes, and typing paper. And got my typewriter out of hock for me, me, Lorenzo the Magnificent.'

The pity of it was that Lorenzo believed that he was the greatest. He had believed it since he was eighteen. The world owed him a living because the world was going to benefit. The world, as typified by Forry Ackerman, owed it to him.

Lorenzo Dummock had said he would do anything, even suck cock if he had to, so he could pursue the call of Apollo. He would do anything except work. Work degraded him, tired him, took precious time from his writing. It was all right for Hulia to work, she should support him while he wrote. Too bad Hulia's asthma and occasional fits of hysteria kept her from holding a steady job. But it couldn't be helped, and if she would suck a few cocks now and then to keep a roof over their head and booze and cigarettes and typing paper at his elbow, what was the harm in that? Forry had turned down an offer by Hulia to blow him. He said that he preferred that she keep the house clean and act as hostess now and then when he had a big party. Hulia had said she would, but it was easier, and more fun, sucking cock. She kept her cunt reserved for Lorenzo, who got killingly jealous at the thought of another man sticking his prick into it. So far, she had done a miserable job as a housekeeper.

Forry turned away from them, swearing that he would kick them out at the first chance, and knowing that he wouldn't. He got into the car, a beat-up 1960 Ford with bald tires, and verified what he had suspected. The fuel indicator was on zero.

Despite this the motor started up and got him one block down Olympic before sputtering out. He walked to the nearest gas station and returned with a canful. Somehow, he never knew how it worked out, he always borrowed their car when it was out of gas.

When he got back to the house, he found Alys Merrie sitting on the sofa in the front room. There was an odor of vomit in the house. Lorenzo had come through again.

'Hello, Alys!' he said, his heart dropping like an elevator with snapped cables. 'What brings you here? And how did you get in?'

'You gave me a key long ago, remember?' she said.

'And I asked for it back, and you gave it to me,' he said.

'So I had a couple of duplicates made in the interim. Aren't you glad to see me, Forry? There was a time . . .'

'Excuse me, I got to attend to something.'

He walked to the foot of the steps and looked up. Halfway to the landing was the nauseating pool. And Hulia had not even bothered to clean it up!

He had returned because he had some vital correspondence to clear up before he went to Wendy's to sleep. But Lorenzo's spoor and Alys Merrie were too much to put up with at this time. He would take off like Seaton after Duquesne.

Alys Merrie thought differently. She was a blonde of medium height and good shape, about forty years old. She had been married, but, on meeting him at a world convention, had, as she put it, 'Gone ape over that divine Forry.' Forry had been amused and flattered for a long time, but she had become a nuisance. He wasn't in love with

72

her, and while her adulation was pleasing, it got sticky after a while. Especially since her husband had threatened to sue him as corespondent.

'The Dummocks are too busy to worry about that puke,' she said. 'I went upstairs to see what was going on, there was so much noise. Would you believe it? That fat-headed Lorenzo was sitting in the chair and Hulia was blowing him! No big deal about that except he was watching her do it and at the same time was taking notes! Taking notes! I wonder if he uses his pen for his prick!'

'Why don't you go back up and watch?' Forry said. 'I have to go, now, Alys. I've been up all night, my car is wrecked, I'm exhausted, I'm worried, and . . . in short, I've had it.'

'Yes, I know all about that.'

He looked at her with amazement. 'You know all about it? Who could have told you?'

'I've been in it from the beginning,' she said. She took a cigarette from her purse, lit it, and looked coolly at him. She knew he allowed no smoking in the house – except in the bedroom upstairs – but she was doing this for a purpose. He decided to ignore the gesture.

'You've been in *what* from the beginning?' he said. Despite his tiredness, he was becoming interested.

'The whole business. Starting so many years ago that you would not believe it. Or, if you did, you'd be frightened. Which you're going to be, anyway, because you'll believe before I'm done.'

He sat down in the chair across the room and said, 'How many years?'

'About ten thousand or so Earth years,' she said.

He was silent for a while. Alys Merrie was a great little kidder when she wasn't mad at him or making love. She knew well how deeply immersed in science-fiction he was – sometimes he thought of himself as the leviathan in the great sea of sci-fi or as a sort of Flying Dutchman of the outer spaceways – and she sometimes poked fun at him about it. This did not seem a likely time for it, however. On the other hand, she just could not be serious.

'Look around you,' she said, waving her cigarette. 'Look at all those wild paintings and photographs. Strange planets, alien forms of life, big-chested, elephant-trunked Martians; winged men; sentient machines; giant insects; synthetic humans; what have you. You've been reading books about weird beings and worlds, and you've collected a monument to science-fiction and fantasy and,

73

incidentally, to yourself. A lifetime of love and labor is represented here.

'You must believe in this exotic otherworld of yours. Otherwise, you would never have gone to such unique lengths to gather the artifacts of the otherworld about you.'

Something was different about Alys Merrie. She had never talked like this before. She had seemed incapable of talking seriously or so fluently.

'Ten thousand years,' she said. 'Would you believe that I'm ten thousand years old? No! What about twelve thousand?'

'Twelve thousand?' he said. 'Come on, Alys. I could believe in ten thousand, but twelve? Don't be ridiculous!'

'I look a hard forty years old, don't I?' she said. 'How about this, Forry?'

It was like watching *She* or *Lost Horizon*, only it was in reverse. Instead of the beautiful young woman wrinkling into ghastly old age, it was a case of a woman unwrinkling, becoming a beautiful young girl. Helen Gahagan and Jane Wyatt should have had it so good.

He wished his heart could beat faster. Then he wouldn't shake so much. So it was true. Everything he had read and dreamed about was true! Well, maybe not everything. But at least some of it was true.

'Who, and what, are you?' he said. The room was beginning to seem a little fuzzy, and the illustrations by Paul, Finlay, St John, Bok, and the rest of the wild crew had taken on three dimensions. He must be in a state of slight shock.

'Do you like it?' Alys said.

'Of course,' Forry said. 'But you didn't answer my question.'

'I am a, uh, let's say, a Toc,' she said. 'We are the enemies of the Ogs. You met some of them last night. Fred Pao, Diana Rumbow, Panchita Pocyotl. And Woolston Heepish.'

# 13

'Heepish!' he almost screamed. 'You mean Heepish isn't human?'

'We're not only *not* human,' she said. 'We're extraterrestrial. Extra-solar system. More. Extra-Galactic. The home of the Tocs is on the fourth planet circling a star in the Andromeda galaxy.'

He thought, I've always been a lucky man. I wanted only to work in science-fiction, and I was able to make my living out of it. I wanted to be the greatest collector of science-fiction and fantasy in the world, and I did that as naturally and as easily as a snail grows a shell. I need a job and a publisher wants to put out a series of horror-movie magazines for children, and who else is more capable or more willing to edit those? I have known the greats of this field, I have been their good friend, I have seen the first men land on the moon, and I hope to see the first men land on Mars before I die. I have been lucky.

But now, this! I would have rejected this as a dream that only a lunatic could believe to be true, even if I have fantasized it many many times. The beings from outer space make contact with Earthlings through me!

That was not exactly true, of course. If what she said was correct, the extees had been in contact with Earthlings for ten thousand years. But had they revealed themselves to any Earthmen before? That was the important thing.

'You're getting too excited, Forry,' she said. 'I know you have a thousand questions bubbling in your mind. But you'll get things straighter and quicker if you'll just listen quietly to my story. Okay? Good! Lean back and be a good boy and listen.'

There was a planet the size and shape of Earth rotating around a Sol-type sun on the edge of the Andromeda galaxy, which was 800,000 light years distant from Earth. The sky was a blaze of luminous gas and giant stars shining through the gas. The planet of the Tocs had no moon, hence was tideless.

The fifth planet out had two small moons but no seas in which tides could occur. This was the dying world of the Ogs, an evil race.

'Geeze!' Forry thought, and the extent of his excitement could be gauged by his use of the mild expletive. He abhorred the use, even in his mind, of the most dilute of expletives.

'Geeze! This is just like Gernsback! Or Early Campbell!'

The Tocs and the Ogs were not human beings. They were amphibious creatures who passed back and forth from a state of pure energy to that of matter. They formed configurations of bound energy in one condition and configurations of matter in the other. Their shape depended on that which they wished to imitate – or to create. But they did have limitations of size and shape. The smallest body that could be formed was about the size of a large fox or, if they took to the air, a large bat. When they existed as the smaller animals, they carried the energy excess in an invisible form as a sort of exhaust trail. Or perhaps the analogy could be energy packed into an intangible and transparent suitcase.

'What is your true shape?' Forry said.

'You were not to talk,' Alys said, flashing white teeth. She looked so beautiful and so young that he felt a pang of desire. Or was it an ache for his own lost youth?

'We have no true shape, unless you would call the shape we use the most our true one. I suppose you could, since long utility of a particular shape results in a certain "hardening" of that shape. It becomes more difficult to change it as time goes on. And it requires more energy to keep it in a nonhuman form. So, since most of us have been in the human shape for so long, you might say that that is our true shape.'

The Ogs and the Tocs had come into contact when space travel was invented. Neither used rockets or antigravitational machines. They traveled from one place in space to another by means of a very peculiar device. That is, it was peculiar from the human viewpoint.

The device was made of a synthetic metal formed into the shape of a large goblet or chalice. That particular form was required because only that form could gather, or focus, the mental energies of a Mover. Perhaps a closer translation of the Toc word would be Captain. The Captain was the only person who could activate the device so that the Tocs could be teleported from one point in space to another.

'Why would the Captain be the only one able to activate the device – this chalice?' Forry said.

'That is the limitation of this device, let us call it the Grail,' Alys said. 'It has a certain superficial resemblance to the grail of your

76

medieval myths, although the inner surface has a geometry that would be alien, even terrifying, to human eyes.

'The Grail is matter, but it is activated only by a certain rare type of energy radiation. Of brainwave radiation, I suppose you would call it, but there is more to it than that. Anyway, the Grail, to act as a spaceship, or a teleport, must be controlled by a Mover, or Captain. And there were only about a hundred Captains born for every million of us born.'

'Born?' Forry said, his eyebrows raising. 'How can an energy configuration be born?'

She waved her hand impatiently and said, 'I am speaking by analogy only. If I have to explain every detail of an exceedingly complex culture, we'll be here for twenty years. Let me talk.'

The Ogs had discovered their Grails and found their Captains the same time as the Tocs. There was travel between the two planets almost at once and war a little later. The Ogs were evil and wanted to enslave the Tocs.

Forry had some mental reservations about this. He would wait until he had heard the Ogs' side before he judged.

The Tocs repulsed the Ogs with heavy losses on both sides. Finally, there was peace. The Tocs and the Ogs then turned their attentions to other worlds. Since distance meant nothing to the Grail, since a hundred thousand light years could be traversed as swiftly as a mile, that is, instantaneously, the universe was open to both races.

But with the billions of habitable planets in the universe, and the limited number of Captains, only a few could be explored. Earth was one of them, and about a thousand Tocs had come here. Almost immediately, the Ogs had sent an expedition here also. The peace did not extend to planets outside their system, so the Ogs had no compunctions about attacking the Tocs.

The Ogs and Tocs had waged a mutually disastrous war. They had destroyed each other's Grail and killed each other's Captains. And so they were marooned on Earth.

'We lived *among* the humans but not *of* them,' Alys said. 'Our ability to take different forms gave rise to a number of superstitions about the supernatural origins of vampires, werewolves, fairies, and what have you. We Tocs were the basis of the good fairies, although we changed into animal shape, or other shapes, quite often. But we weren't hostile to human beings, that is, if they followed the proper ethics we weren't.'

Over the ten thousand years, the War, the occasional killing of human beings, and suicide cut the original number of about two thousand Togs and Ogs down to about a hundred each. However, every Toc or Og whose material form was slain was not dead. He became an energy configuration again and could regain material form. But this process took a long time on Earth because the magnetic conditions here were not the same as in the mother system.

'That accounts for ghosts?' Forry said.

'Yes. Human beings don't have ghosts. When they die, they are forever dead. But a Toc or Og who has died in material form needs to attach himself to a locale where he has both the optimum magnetic conditions and human beings. He has to, shall we say, "feed" off the energy of human beings. And when he has gained enough form, in a phase which you humans call ectoplasm, he needs blood or sex to get a completely material body. The Tocs need sex and the Ogs need blood.'

She paused and then said, 'One of us recently regained corporeal form by contact with Herald Childe. She literally fucked herself into flesh. Of course, she was able to do it far more swiftly with Childe than she would have with one who was completely a human being.'

# 14

'What the hell does that mean?' said Forry, who almost never swore.

'I mean that Childe is the only Captain in existence. But he doesn't know it as yet.'

'Why not?'

'Because he was born half-human and raised by human parents. Because a Captain has a delicate psychic constitution and must be handled delicately until he has fully matured. Childe is a fully mature man in the physical sense, but he is a baby in regard to his psychic powers.'

'Just one minute,' Forry said. 'I don't want to digress, but if you beings can come back to material life after being killed, why haven't these Captains that were killed come back to life?'

'Some did and were killed by one side or the other because their existence could not be kept secret. Others never made it because conditions weren't right. You see, if we had a Captain and a Grail, we could not only return to our home world. We could also bring all our departed comrades back into corporeality. The Toc or Og in his pure energy-complex phase is a rather mindless being. He has some intelligence, but the main reason he gets back to matter is that he has a drive to do so, an instinct. He wanders around until he happens to come across a locale with the proper setup for reconverting him. And reconversion takes a long long time generally.'

'Pardon the interruption,' Forry said.

If he had not seen that transformation from middle age to youth, he would have thought he was experiencing the world's biggest hoax. But he was convinced. He was actually talking face to face, with an extraterrestrial. One that would have made the strangest creature of science-fiction, or even those in *Weird Tales* magazine, rather mundane.

He thought, In a sense, she's telling me the story of the Martians and Venusians waging an underground war for control of Earth. Hugo, you should be here! Oh, boy, if I could just flip a switch and let the sci-fi fans and the Count Dracula Society in on this!

And then he sobered. If this was true, and he believed it was, this was no mere fiction story or child's delight. It was a deadly war.

'Childe?' he said.

'Let's go back to 1788,' she said. 'To the birth of the male who would become George Gordon, Lord Byron, the famous, if not great, English poet. At the time he was born, of course, no one, including us, knew that he would become world-famous. Nor did we have any way of predicting whether he would become a Captain or just another human being. Or just another Toc.'

'I'm bursting with questions,' he said, smiling. 'But I refrain.'

'He was our first birth,' she said. 'On Toc, where conditions are optimum, births are very rare. That is, births from a copulation between, or among, our energy configuration phases do not happen often. But then that is counterbalanced by our lack of a death rate.

'Here on Earth, we had never succeeded in producing an infant in the energy configuration. Then a Captain was reconverted into material form. One of us had the idea of preserving his genetic abilities in case he should get killed, which he was later on. The Captain happened to be living near the Byrons at that time, and he became the lover of Lady Byron with the purpose of impregnating her. There were a hundred of us, almost our full complement, gathered together nearby the night she conceived George. I suppose it is the only case, except one, where a hundred people copulated to produce one baby. We poured our mental energies into Lady Byron, and we succeeded. Coexisting with the fusion of sperm and ovum was the creation of an energy embryo. This embryo was attached, no, was fused with the body of the infant Byron. You might say that he was the only human being up to then who actually had a soul.'

'Pardon me, but how did that energy embryo develop? Did it become a separate entity or . . .?'

'It fuses with the nervous system and becomes one with the corporeal entity. Not identical but similar. It survives after the death of the body.

'However, this creation of an energy baby requires much outpouring of energy on our part. At the same time that we were concentrating our mental energies, we were fucking like mad corporeally. It was probably the biggest gang-bang in history, if you will pardon such language, Forry dear. I know you don't like to use *dirty* words or especially to hear them.

'Unfortunately, though the baby grew up to have some remarkable talents, it did not develop the psychic abilities of a Captain. Not that that would have done much good, anyway, because we did not have the Grail. But we hoped to make the metal for one; we had been creating the metal, bit by bit, over thousands of years. On Toc we could have done it in a year, but here, where the minerals are scarce and the materials for building the *potentializers* are even more rare, we took an agonizingly long time getting what we needed. Then the Ogs made a raid and stole what metal we had.

'They knew that Byron was to be our Captain. They moved in, became acquainted with him, and we could do little about it. Then they abandoned him when they found out that he lacked the Captaincy.

'We were in despair for a while. But Byron still had the genetic potentiality for a Captain, and we decided to take advantage of that. If he couldn't be a Captain, perhaps his child could be.'

'Childe?' Forry said, ever alert for the chance to pun.

She nodded and said, 'Exactly. We got specimens of his sperm by a method I won't go into and froze it. Not with ice or liquid hydrogen but with an energy configuration. And we waited.

'We waited while our enemies, the Ogs, obtained more metal, enough to make a Grail. Then we chose a woman with suitable genetic qualities, humanly speaking, because those have to be considered, too. You wouldn't want the Captain to be an inferior physical or mental specimen. And we deliberately settled on Mrs Childe because of the name. And its association with Byron, too. After all, we use human languages and so we think something like humans. Only like, not exactly as.'

'Thus, Herald Childe from the Childe Harold?'

'If you said H-E-R-A-L-D, yes. Herald. The Child that Heralds the rebirth of our Toc energy ghosts, their materialization. And our return to the Promised Land of our native planet. The dead shall rise and we shall cross the river Zion into the Land of Beulah, if I can mix up a few quotations. You get the idea.'

'And what about Childe and the Grail?' Forry said.

Alys Merrie opened her mouth to reply, but she shut it when someone beat at the door and shouted.

# 15

At noon, the ringing of the doorbell awakened Childe. He staggered out into the front room, past Sybil, who was still sleeping, and threw open the front door. A gust of rain wet him and covered the three men standing on his porch. He realized immediately that he should have been more cautious, but by then it was too late. The first man stepped inside, holding a spray can. Childe held his breath and ran towards his bedroom, where he kept a gun. He stopped when the man called, 'Childe! Your wife!'

The second man was by Sybil with a knife at her throat. The third, Fred Pao or his twin, held an air gun.

The first man sprayed a gas over Sybil just as she opened her eyes and said, 'Wha . . .?'

She fell back asleep, and Pao said, 'It won't hurt her. Now your turn, Mr Childe.'

He could still run for the bedroom, he thought. But these men would cut Sybil's throat if they thought they had anything, or nothing, to gain by it. Of course, he might be able to kill all three of them with his gun, but what good would that do Sybil? On the other hand, if he surrendered, wouldn't he and Sybil be as good as dead?

He did not know. That was the paralyzing factor. He did not know. And from what had passed between Vivienne and Hindarf he surmised that he was regarded as something special.

'All right,' he said. 'I surrender.'

The man with the spray can approached him and shot the vapor in his face. He wanted to hold his breath, but it was foolish putting off the inevitable. After glancing at his wristwatch, he breathed in.

It was thirty minutes later when he awoke. He was lying on a comfortable bed and looking up at a canopy. He turned his head and saw Sybil beside him. She was still unconscious. He got out of bed with some effort, noting that he had a slight headache and a brassy tongue and gums. His teeth felt enlarged.

Their prison was a single bedroom and a bathroom. There was one door for entrance.

Sybil woke up. She lay there for a while and then got out of bed.

She went to him, and he put his arm around her and said, 'I'm sorry about this. If I had made you leave, you wouldn't be in this mess.'

'That can't be helped,' she said. 'Do you think that we'll ever get out of this? I wish I knew what these people wanted.'

'We should find out sooner or later,' he said. He released her and prowled around the room. There was a large mirror fixed in the wall above the dresser and another wall-high mirror on the opposite side of the room. He supposed that these were one-way.

An hour passed. Sybil had quit trying to talk and had started to read, of all things, a mystery novel she found in a bookcase. He investigated again with the idea of using something to help them get out. He observed that the door was heavy steel and was set tightly against the wall. It swung outward.

An hour and a half after awakening, the door was opened. Pao and two men entered. Sybil spoke to one: 'Plugger!'

Plugger was a tall, well-built, dark-skinned man. His hands were long and narrow with long tapering fingers. These were covered with small protuberances, a feature Sybil had not described.

'Our enemies – and yours – were moving in fast,' Pao said. 'That is why we had to take you two away. I am sorry; we're all sorry. But it had to be done. Otherwise, you would have fallen into the hands of the Tocs.'

'Tocs?' Childe said.

'Everything will be explained,' Pao said. 'Very quickly. Meanwhile, we require your presence elsewhere.

'And Sybil?'

'She will have to stay here. But she won't be harmed.'

Childe kissed Sybil and said, 'I'll be back. I don't think they intend us any evil. Not now, anyway.'

He watched Plugger shut the door. There was a button in its middle; when this was pressed, an unlocking mechanism was activated. Childe reached out and pressed the button, and the door swung out swiftly.

Pao said, 'What are you doing?' and pressed the button to shut the door.

'I just wanted to see how it worked,' Childe said.

They started down the hall, which was wide and luxuriously carpeted and furnished. He stopped after a few steps. He had been right. The mirror was a one-way device. He could see Sybil still standing in the middle of the room, her hands clenched by her sides.

He decided to see how valuable he was to them.

'I'd like that mirror turned off,' he said. 'I don't like being spied on.'

Pao hesitated and then said, 'Very well.'

He pressed a button on the side of the mirror and it darkened.

'I'd like the other mirror turned off, too,' Childe said.

'I'll see it's done,' Pao said. 'Come along now.'

Childe followed him with the other two men behind him. At the end of the hall, they turned left into another hall and halfway down that turned right into a very large room. This looked like the salon of a millionaire's house as constructed for a movie set. There was a magnificent concert piano at the far end and very expensive furniture, perhaps genuine Louis XV pieces, around the room. A peculiar feature, however, was the glass or transparent metal cube set in the middle of the room. Inside this was a slender-legged dark-red wooden table on top of which was a silvery goblet. Or half a goblet. One side seemed to be complete, but the other was missing. It was as if a shears had cut through the cup part of the goblet at a forty-five-degree angle.

Pao led Childe to the transparent cube and motioned to a man to bring a chair. Childe looked around. There were six exits, some of them broad enough for three men to go through abreast. There were also about fifty men and women in the room, a large number of them between him and the exits. All were dressed in tails and gowns. Pao and his two men were the only ones in business clothes. He recognized Panchita Pocyotl and Vivienne Mabcrough. Vivienne was dressed in a scarlet floor-length formal gown with a deep V almost to her navel. Her pale skin and auburn hair contrasted savagely with the flaming gown. She was holding a big ostrich fan. Seeing his eyes on her, she smiled.

The crowd had been talking when he entered but the conversation softened as he was brought before the cube. Now Pao held up his hand, and the voices died away. A man brought a chair with three legs, a heavy wooden thing with a symbol carved into the back. The symbol was a delta with one end stuck into the open mouth of a rampant fish.

'Please sit down,' Pao said.

Childe sat down in the chair and leaned against its back. He could feel the alto-relief of the carved symbol pressing into his back. At the same time, the dull silver of the goblet inside the cube became bright and shimmery. The brightness increased until it glowed as if it were about to melt.

A murmur of what sounded to him like awe ran through the people.

Pao smiled and said, 'We would appreciate it if you would concentrate on the goblet, Herald Childe.'

'Concentrate how?' Childe said.

'Just look at it. Examine it thoroughly. Let it fill your mind. You will know what I mean.'

Childe shrugged. Why not? The procedure and the goblet had aroused his curiosity, and their intentions did not seem sinister. Certainly, he was being treated far better than when he had been a prisoner in Igescu's.

He sat in the chair and stared at the shining goblet. It had a broad base with small raised figures, the outlines of which were fuzzy. After a while, as he studied them, they became clear. They were men and women, naked, and animals engaged in a sexual orgy. Set here and there among them were goblets like that at which he looked, except that these were complete. There was a curious scene in which a tiny woman was halfway into a large goblet while a creature that looked like the Werewolf of London, as played by Henry Hull, rammed a long dick into her asshole. At one side of the base, almost out of view, was a man emerging from a goblet. His legs were still within the cup, but his stiff dong was out and was being squeezed by the tentacle of a creature that seemed to be a six-legged octopus with human hermaphroditic organs. While it was jacking off the man in the goblet, it was also fucking itself.

Childe did not know what the scene represented, but it seemed to him that it had something to do with fecundity. Not with fecundity in the sense of begetting children but of . . .

He almost grasped the sense of the figures and their play, but it danced away.

The goblet stem was slender. A snake-like thing of silver coiled around it, its head flattening out to become the underpart of the cup. Its two eyes, distorted, were the only dark spots on the bright silver of the goblet.

The outside of the cup, except for the serpent's head, was bare. But the inside bore some raised geometrical figures that shifted as he looked at them. Sometimes he could pin them down for a half a second and the figures began to make sense, even if they were totally unfamiliar.

The goblet shone even more brilliantly. The room became quieter, and then, suddenly, he could hear the breathing of everyone in the room, except for himself, and, far away, the impact of rain on the roof and the walls of the house and, even more distantly, the roar of waters down the street outside.

There was a hissing he could not at first identify. It was so weak, so remote. And then he knew. He did not have to turn his head to look, and it would have done no good if he had. The thing was hidden under Vivienne's dress. It had slid out and was dangling between her legs. Its little bearded mouth was open, the tongue flickering out, and it was hissing with rage or lust. Or, perhaps, some other emotion. Awe?

The light from the goblet became more intense. Surprisingly, he could look at it without pain. Its whiteness seemed to drill into his eyes and flood his brain. The interior of his skull was white; his brain was a glowing jewel.

There was a collective intake of breath, and the light went out. The darkness that followed was painful. He felt as if something very much beloved had died. His life was empty; he had no reason to live.

He wept.

# 16

When he was finished sobbing – and he still did not know why he had felt so bereaved – he looked up. The people were not talking, but they were making some noise as they shifted around. Also, several were passing through the crowd and serving a liquid in small goblets. The people drank it with one swallow and then put their goblets back on to the large silver trays.

Pao appeared from behind him with a tray on which stood a goblet filled with a dark liquid, and several sandwiches. The bread was coarse and black.

'Drink and then eat,' Pao said.

'And if I don't?'

Pao looked stricken, but he shrugged his shoulders and said, 'This is one thing that we can't compel you to do. But I swear by my mother planet that the food and drink will not harm you.'

Childe looked at the goblet again. It was not quite as dull as it had been a moment ago. It flickered when he looked at it. When he looked away, but could still see it out of the corner of his eye, it became dull once more.

'When will I find out what all this means?' Childe said.

'Perhaps during the ceremony. It is better that you . . . remember.'

'Remember?'

Pao did not offer to explain. Childe smelled the liquid. Its odor was winey, but there was an unfamiliar underodor (was there such a word?) to it. The underodor evoked a flashing image of an infinite black space with stars here and there and then another image of a night sky with sheets of white fire and giant red, blue, yellow, garnet, emerald, and purple stars filling the sky. And there was a fleeting landscape of red rock with mushroom-shaped buildings of white and red stone, trees that looked inverted, with their branches on the ground and their roots feeding on the air, and a thin band with scarlet, pale green, and white threads, something like a Saturn's ring, arcing across the sky near the horizon.

He drained the tiny goblet with one gulp and, feeling hungry immediately afterward, ate the sandwiches. The meat tasted like beef with blue cheese.

When the goblets had been passed around, and everybody was standing as if waiting for something to happen – which they were, Childe supposed – Pao raised his hands. He spoke in a loud voice: 'The Childe must have power!'

That was a funny way to refer to him, Childe thought. *The* Childe?

The crowd answered in a loud chorus, 'The Childe must have power!'

Pao said, 'There is but one way in which The Childe may gain this power!'

The people echoed, 'There is but one way in which The Childe may gain power!'

'And grow!'

'And grow!'

'And become a man!'

'And become a man!'

'And become our Captain!'

'And become our Captain!'

'And lead us to our long lost home!'

'And lead us to our long lost home!'

'And permit us to triumph over our enemies, the Tocs!'

'And permit us to triumph over our enemies, the Tocs!'

'Through the nothingness and the utter cold he will lead us!'

There was more, none of which made any sense to Childe except for the reference to their enemies, the Tocs. These must be the people of whom he had so far met only three. The three who had rescued him from Vivienne and reproached her for breaking the truce.

The liquor was making him feel very heady by then. And the food had infused him with strength. He looked at the goblet, which glowed as if his gaze beamed radium at it.

Pao finally finished his chanting. Immediately, the crowd became noisy. They started talking and laughing. And they were also stripping off their clothes. Panchita Pocyotl shed her gown, revealing that she wore nothing under it except long stockings held up by huge scarlet garters. Vivienne was not far behind her; she wore a garter belt and stockings. The snake-thing had withdrawn; her auburn bush looked very attractive.

Pao, naked, his skinny dick dangling halfway down between his thighs, said, 'Would you please undress, Captain?'

Childe, feeling dizzy, rose. He said, 'Captain?'

'You will know what I mean – I hope,' Pao said.

Childe remembered with a pang of dread his treatment at the hands of the enormously fat Mrs Grasatchow when he was a prisoner in Igescu's house.

He said, 'Am I to be abused?'

'No one would think of that now,' Pao said. 'Vivienne made a very bad mistake, and if we did not need her so much, we might have killed her. But she was overcome by your power, and that is a reasonable excuse for her actions. Nevertheless, she will not be permitted to touch you tonight.'

Childe, looking at the naked and superbly shaped woman, felt his penis rising. The liquid seemed to have gone down warmly to the place behind his navel and there caught fire. The blaze spread out, up, and down, but mainly down. The base of his cock was rammed with a boiling and heavy liquid metal; it expanded upwards, filling out his cock, lifting it up, and making it throb.

He said, 'All right,' and he undressed.

Pao took his clothes and left the room. Childe, standing there, felt foolish, and so he sat down. The others seemed to know what was expected of them; they began embracing and caressing each other, standing up, or lying down on the floor, or on the sofas. They were not putting their whole hearts into their love-making, however; they were waiting for someone or something.

Pao returned. He walked up to Childe, took his hand, and said, 'Your blessing, Captain.'

He placed his long slim peter on Childe's upturned palm, and the dead worm came to life. It became red and swollen and rose up off the hand as if launched. Pao backed away and bowed and kissed Childe's hand where his peter had lain.

'I thank you, Captain,' he said.

There was a scramble among the couples after that. They arranged themselves in a double line in an order of precedence which they seemed to know well. There was no quarreling or struggling to get ahead of one another.

The first two in line were Panchita Pocyotl and a big blond man with Scandinavian features. They stood before Childe, between him and the goblet in the cube.

The man said, 'Your pardon, Captain,' and took Childe's hand and closed the fingers around his half-erect dong. At the touch, the big-knobbed dong filled up like a blimp being engorged with gas. It lay hard and throbbing in Childe's hand, and a small drop of fluid oozed out of the slit in the glans. The man stepped back and Panchita got down on her knees and took Childe's penis in one hand and kissed it on the head and the shaft. Then she arose, looked once into his eyes with her large luminous dark-brown eyes, and withdrew with the man.

Childe watched them. They walked to a sofa and lay down on it. Panchita spread her legs out and over his shoulders, and he inserted himself into the thick black glossy bush and began pumping. His red Swedish ass went faster and faster and then, suddenly, both groaned and writhed. After they had come, they lay quiescent and then, a few minutes later, he was fucking her dog fashion.

This excited Childe, who wanted the next woman kissing his cock to continue. But she backed away, murmuring, 'Thank you, Captain,' and went away with her squat Indian partner and his thick stubby penis.

The couples came quickly, the men laying their dongs in his hands and the women kissing or licking his cock. There were exceptions, however. Some of the men also got down and kissed or even sucked briefly on him, and some of the women took his hand and placed it on their cunts.

Childe had been slightly repulsed by some of this at the beginning. But as more couples approached him, as more couples began fucking or sucking, he accepted it as something natural to him. He began thinking of it as his due, and then as something old and familiar. The flashes of the exotic and extraterrestrial landscapes occurred more frequently, each time coincident with the placing of a dong in his hand or the slide of lips over the head and shaft of his cock.

The goblet had increased its illumination during this ceremony. As each couple passed, it shone a trifle more brightly. And the white glow in his skull was exceeded only by the hot whiteness in his penis. It was so strong a sensation, he was disappointed when he looked down and did not see glans and shaft radiating with a white light.

Pao, he noticed, had no steady partner. He wandered around, and when he found a vacant cunt or empty mouth, he filled it. He did not seem to care whether or not the other was male or female. He came each time he rammed his partner with a few strokes, and then he would withdraw his dripping but still rigid dick and go on to the next person.

The only one missing, he suddenly noticed, was Plugger. He had shown up early in the line and given Childe a slight shock when he closed Childe's hand around his warty cock. Childe had felt an increase in the ecstasy building up in him but that was all. He had the feeling that Plugger was withholding, that he had, somehow, turned down his bioelectricity to a minimum. And then Plugger, after briefly fucking his partner but leaving her passed out, had disappeared.

Childe considered this for a second. He had an image of Plugger walking down the hall towards Sybil's room. Was the bastard going to her? And then he forgot about him when the next woman ran her tongue over the head of his penis.

Although the line had been sedate enough, considering the actions of the couples, the people became wild once they had left him. They talked loudly, swore, smacked loudly when kissing or sucking each other off, and filled the room with the slap-slap of wet cocks driving against wet cunts or into wet assholes. They groaned and moaned or screamed with the ecstasy of orgasm oncoming or occurring. And the air was heavy and musky with the odors of sweating bodies, lubricating fluid, and sperm.

The fantastically beautiful Vivienne, although denied touching him, was taking advantage of her liberty with her fellows. She was standing bent over, sucking on a big black's cock while Pao thrust his dick into her anus and the snake-thing looped under Pao's balls and slid back and forth into his anus. They all seemed to come at once, judging from their writhings and shakings. The black's cock dwindled to a half-erection and came out of the mouth of Vivienne, who swallowed the gism. Pao's dick withdrew and was at half-mast, dripping. The snake-thing left Pao's ass reluctantly with its mouth still vomiting spermatic fluid and coiling and uncoiling in the final spasms of orgasm.

At that moment, the last woman in line quit tickling his glans with her tongue. Pao, his cock beginning to rise again but still expelling the gray fluid, walked across the room to him. Childe looked at him with a mute appeal. He was close to coming, and his peter was throbbing in the air. In one corner of his mind, he noted the goblet had begun to pulse. The whiteness flared and dimmed, flared and dimmed.

Just before Pao reached him, he made the connection with full awareness. The goblet was emitting pulses of light in phase with the throbbings of his dong.

Pao took Childe's hand and lifted it. His dick rose so high it almost

91

touched his navel. Childe's own organ seemed to lurch, and its head touched his belly. The throbbings increased, the warm gray tide in his testicles and ducts rose more swiftly, and the glory in him threatened to shoot out.

'Come on!' he said fiercely to Pao.

Pao waved his hand, and Childe understood that he was to take his pick.

Childe looked quickly around. He had a superb choice, because there were very few women in the room who were not extraordinarily beautiful.

Childe said, 'Vivienne!'

Pao was startled and opened his mouth, apparently intending to protest. But he closed it, and crooked a finger at Vivienne.

Vivienne was startled, too. She pointed a finger at herself and mouthed, 'Me?'

Pao nodded and gestured for her to come a-running. She did so with the snake-thing flopping between her legs, banging into her knees and protesting against the treatment. When Vivienne got to Childe, she dropped on her knees and said, 'Forgive me, my Captain.'

Then she started to suck on the end of his cock. The ecstasy came in slow waves, and from the inside of his navel to his knees he became ice.

He managed to gasp at Pao, 'Jerk that thing out!'

'What?' Pao said.

'Pull that thing out of her cunt! Quick!'

Pao got down behind Childe and reached through his legs and grabbed the snake-thing, which was trying to wrap itself around Childe's thigh. Apparently it intended to climb up and into Childe's asshole, although it was doubtful that it was long enough to reach its goal. But Pao grabbed it behind its head and gave a savage yank.

Vivienne fell apart.

Childe stood with her head between his hands and his penis in her mouth. The eyes stared up at him with a violet fire, and the lips and tongue kept on sucking and thrusting. The other parts of her body, having gotten on to their legs, began to scuttle around the room. The big black who had been sucked off by Vivienne picked up the many-legged cunt and stuck it on the end of his cock and began sliding it back and forth. The cunt's legs kicked as if it were having an orgasm.

The goblet's pulses came faster and faster. Childe held the head by the ears and rammed his prick faster and faster between the lips. Its head drove down her throat, backed out until it almost left those beautiful lips, and then rammed in until the hairs around his cock were crushed against her lips.

Faster and faster. Brighter and brighter. Pulse and ecstasy.

The ice turned to fire. He spurted with a scream and a writhing that was so violent he almost dropped the head. His pubis was against her nose and his dong was far down her throat. He came and came, and the goblet glowed as if it were in the heart of the sun.

Pao got down underneath the head and swallowed the gism that fell down her throat and out the open neck.

The others scrambled to catch the drops that Pao had missed. They rolled him away, and stuck their heads under Vivienne's, and then they were pushed away. Those who could not get any directly ran their fingers over the lips or down the mouths of those who had been lucky and got the stuff second-hand. Some tasted it and then rubbed the residue over their cunts or pricks.

Childe quit shaking and spurting. The goblet's light waned swiftly, and soon it had only a faint glow.

He pulled Vivienne's head off his peter and threw it to Pao, saying, 'Now you can put her together again. I had my revenge.'

He sat down and stared dully at the goblet. He felt very tired.

The people crowded around and spoke in awed tones. At first, he did not understand what they were talking about. When he heard a woman say, 'It did grow, just a little, but it grew!' he saw what they were marveling at.

The incomplete side of the cup of the goblet was now half-filled in. It had grown more of the metal.

'You are indeed the Captain and The Childe,' Pao said, holding Childe's limp cock in his hand. 'But you are no longer a child.'

Childe understood what he was saying, although he did not know the details. During that last explosion of orgasm, he had seen many things on the screen of his mind. Somehow, this experience had tapped a racial memory. No, not racial. That was not the correct term. A genetic memory was closer to an exact definition.

# 17

Forry Ackerman jumped when the poundings came on his door. He opened the door without checking on the identity of the visitor, a lack of precaution indicating his upset condition.

A tall good-looking man with yellow hair and dark blue eyes stood there. Two other men were with him.

He said, 'I'm Hindarf. This is Bellow and this is Grunder. We're friends, old friends, of Alys Merrie. We'd like to come in.'

'No smoking,' Forry said and then remembered that Alys was puffing on one cigarette after another.

He let them in and closed the door. Two sat down without asking his permission; Hindarf stood in the middle of the room as if he intended to dominate it. And he did.

'I'm here to carry out the rest of our plan,' he said.

'What plan?' Forry said.

He looked around the room. It had always seemed the center of the universe, this room. It contained illustrations from all over the cosmos by men who had never left the planet Earth in the flesh. Memos from Mars. To others, it appeared weird, but to him it was home.

Now it was shifting from reality, slipping its moorings. The very intrusion of genuine alienness rendered this place alien. The aliens were the real people, and the products of imagination were fake. Contrary to what he had always maintained, reality was more real than fantasy.

'You must be wondering why you've been chosen,' Hindarf said. 'Why should we bring in an Earthling in our battle against the Ogs? Why do we need you in our effort to recapture the Captain?'

Forry bent his head and looked at them from under raised eyebrows. He drawled, 'Yes. I had been wondering about that. Many are called but Fu are Cho-sen, as the Korean said.'

Hindarf did not smile, but he did not look puzzled either. He said, 'There are some Earthlings who have what we call *resonance*. Through the chance of genetics, they are born with a psychic affinity, or a psychophysical complex, which generates what, for want of a better term, we call *white noise*. This vibration is quite in phase with those radiated by the Tocs. It makes the Earthling immediately sympathetic and empathic with the Tocs, and, conversely, it generates disturbance and confusion in the minds of the Ogs. But it exists, and its effect is to blank out the vibrations radiated by the Tocs. In other words, we Tocs and Ogs know when we're near each other. We sense it just as a lion downwind from an antelope smells it. But when one of the resonant white-noise generator Earthlings is around, the Ogs can't sense us.'

Forry put his fingertips together to form a church steeple. He said, 'I've never been one to make everything black or white. There is much more gray in this universe than black or white.'

'Did you ever have a good word to say for the Nazis?' Hindarf said.

'Well, they did get rockets launched and that led to the first men on the Moon.'

Alys Merrie guffawed and said, 'Well, kiss my ass and call me Hitler!'

'Woolston Heepish is a member of the Ogs,' Hindarf said. 'He has not only set himself up as a rival of yours, he has become a caricature of you, and he has stolen from you. Do you think he's more gray than black?'

'Black as the devil's hindbrain,' Forry said. 'Why, just last night . . .!'

Hindarf waved his hand impatiently and said, 'I know. The question is, will you help us? It will be dangerous. But it will be less dangerous for us if you accompany us. We intend to rescue Childe. He is a prisoner of the Ogs. And the emanations from the house today indicate that he's participating in a grail-growing ceremony. He probably doesn't know what he's doing, but that makes no difference. He is doing what they want him to do.'

'Aren't there any other Earthlings you know who could go with you?' Forry said. He remembered some of his youthful fantasies in which he had been the focus of attention from the secret band of Martians and Venusians operating in an underground struggle for control of Earth. Generally, in his fantasies, he had been on the side of the Martians. There was something sinister, damp, toadstooly, and creepycrawly about the Venusians. All that rain . . . Now that he thought about it, the deluge of the past seven days had turned Los Angeles into a Venus such as the sci-fi writers had projected back in the good old days of *Science Wonder Stories* and *Astounding*.

'No,' Hindarf said. 'There are none available in this area, and none anywhere who can generate white noise to compare with yours.'

'This may seem irrelevant to you at this moment,' Forry said, 'but why does Heepish steal from me?'

'Because he wants your stuff for the collection he intends to take to the planet of the Ogs. He's a greedy and short-sighted person, and that is why he's stolen a few things from you instead of waiting to take the whole collection just before he leaves.'

'What?' Forry said shrilly. 'The whole collection?'

'Oh, yes,' Alys Merrie said, blowing smoke at him. 'He has planned on emptying your house and your garage. He can do it in a few minutes, you know, if he can get a Captain to do it for him. The collection would be moved to a huge room in a barn behind the present headquarters of the Ogs. Then, when the Captain moves all the Ogs to their home planet, he will also take the collection. Which, by the way, will consist of many of Earth's art treasures in addition to artifacts and books and so forth, for the Og museums.'

'You can visit our planet, if you wish,' Hindarf said. 'And you might as well have Heepish's collection too. It won't do him any good after he's dead.'

'Dead?'

Hindarf nodded and said, 'Of course. We plan to kill every Og.'

Forry did not like the idea of killing, even if Heepish did deserve it. But the thought of going to an alien planet, one so far away that it was not even in this galaxy! He alone, of all men, would voyage to another world! He had wanted to be the first man on the Moon and the first man on Mars when he was a child and then that dream had glimmered away. He wouldn't even be able to go to those places as a tourist. And now, he was offered a free ticket to a planet far more alien and weird than the Moon or Mars could ever be. Under a strange sun on an unimaginably exotic world!

'I can come back any time I wish?' he said. 'I wouldn't want to leave Los Angeles forever, you know. I have my collection and all my wonderful friends.'

'No trouble,' Hindarf said.

'I must warn you, if it involves anything strenuous, I'll be handicapped,' Forry said. 'My heart . . .'

'Alys has told us all about that,' Hindarf said.

Forry's eyes widened. 'Everything?'

'Just the medical aspects,' Hindarf said.

'All right then,' Foffy said. 'I'll help you. But just as a white noise generator. You can't ask me to take part in any killing.'

The three men and Alys smiled.

Forry smiled, too, but he was not sure that he was not making a pact with the devil. It seemed that the Og really were evil, but then the Tocs might not be so good, either. It could be a case of one band of devils fighting another.

# 18

Childe awoke with a feeling of emptiness and of shame.

He looked at Sybil, who was sleeping by his side, and then he stared upward for a long time. Something had happened to him last night, or he presumed it was last night, since he did not know what time it was. His wristwatch was gone.

As if a key had been turned in him, unlocking a memory or releasing a programmed tape, he had gone through that ceremony without a false step or being told, really, what to do next.

When he had evoked that pulsing light, he had felt an ecstasy that was superior, in some undefinable way, to that of sexual orgasm. It was difficult to untangle the sexual from the photonic, but a part of the glory had been from that goblet.

That final incident, the one with Vivienne's unattached head, had seemed at the moment to be fully justified and exquisitely delightful. But this morning it looked ugly and perverted. He could not understand what had possessed him.

The hell of it was, he thought, that the next time he was seated before that goblet, he was likely to do the same thing or something equally uninhibited. He did not fool himself about that.

The worst thing about this was that he was cooperating with people – beings, rather – who were evil.

But when he had been placed before that goblet, he had been unable to refuse to act. In a sense, the goblet had activated him more than he had activated it.

What was supposed to be the final result of this ceremony and of others that would undoubtedly follow it?

He decided that he would refuse to do anything more unless everything was fully explained.

He thought of Sybil. Would she be tortured if he refused to carry out the Ogs' desires? Knowing what he did of them, he could not doubt that they would do whatever they thought was required. And so Sybil would be . . . He shuddered.

Somebody knocked on the door. It was faint because the door was of such thick metal, but he was aware of it. His sense of hearing seemed to be sharper after last night's experiences. He rose, noting that he was naked and not caring, and went to the door. He rapped on it, and the door swung outward. Vivienne was standing there with Pao behind her.

'You people are so technologically advanced, you could find some easier way to get my attention,' he said.

'You indicated you wanted privacy in your room,' Vivienne said. 'So we polarized the one-way windows and turned off the TV monitor and the intercom.'

'That's nice of you,' he said, thinking that they were really trying to sell him on how extremely nice they were. 'Show me where this intercom is, and I'll contact you when I want you. And be sure to keep the other devices off.'

'What the Captain wishes . . .' Pao murmured.

'What I wish now, after a good breakfast, are answers to my questions.'

Pao said, 'Of course,' as if he was amazed that Childe could have any reason to think otherwise.

'I'll see you in ten minutes,' he said. 'You'd better tell me where the breakfast room is. And leave the door unlocked.'

Pao looked embarrassed. He said, 'I'm sorry indeed, my Captain, but you'll have to stay in here. It's for your own safety. There are evil people who want to hurt you. You cannot leave this room. Except for the Grailing, of course.'

'The Grailing?'

'Growing that goblet. The Grail.'

'There is to be more of that?'

'There is.'

'Very well then,' Childe said. 'I'm a prisoner.'

Pao bowed slightly and said, 'A ward, Captain. For your own protection.'

Childe closed the door in their faces and woke up Sybil. She did not want to get out of bed, but he told her he wanted her to hear everything that would be said. He started towards the bathroom but stopped when he saw a hairy pointed head sticking out from under the bed. It looked vaguely like a sleeping black dog about the size of a Great Dane. He rapped it on its wet doggy nose, and it opened its eyes wide.

'What the hell are you and what the hell are you doing under my bed?' he said.

The eyes were dark brown and looked familiar. But the animal that crawled out from under the bed was unfamiliar. Its front part resembled a giant water spaniel, and the back part was monkeylike. It stood up on its semi-human feet and staggered over to a chair and sat down. It leaned its shaggy floppy-eared head on its two paws. The monkey part was hairy but not so hairy it entirely concealed a pair of human testicles and a warty penis.

'I was hungry,' Childe said aloud. 'But seeing you, whatever you are . . .'

He felt repulsed but not scared. The thing did not look dangerous, not, at least, at the moment. Its weariness and its big wet gentle eyes added up to harmlessness.

One thing its presence did for him. It reaffirmed the sense of alienness, of unhumanity, about these people.

Sybil did not seem frightened; he would have expected her to be screaming with hysteria.

He said, 'Was this your bed partner last night, Sybil?'

'Part of the time,' she said.

'There was more than one?'

The only one missing from the ceremony, as far as he knew, was Plugger.

'I don't think so,' she said. 'He seemed to have changed into this about a half hour before we quit.'

He did not have to ask her what they had quit doing.

'He said he was almost emptied,' Sybil said. 'He had been to the three Toc prisoners before he came to me. I suppose he buggered them, I mean, he applied his limp prick to their anuses and shocked them with the only pleasant shock that I know of. Then he came to me.'

Childe did not feel that he was in a position to rebuke her. What good would it do, anyway? She took sex where she found it and enjoyed it. And all the time professing that he was her only true love. The truth was, sex was her only true love. Impersonal sex.

The unbelievable element in this was not so much the metamorphosis of Plugger into this dog-monkey thing as it was her calm acceptance of the metamorphosis. She should have been in a deep state of psychic shock.

'Why did Plugger feel it necessary to stimulate the prisoners?' he said.

'He told me that everybody in the house had to be hooked into the

100

Grailing and that only if the prisoners and I had sex with an Og could this be done.'

A voice spoke from a jade statuette on a table against the wall near the bed: 'Captain, is there anything you want?'

'Yes!' he said, facing the statuette. 'Get this thing out of here! Plugger is making me sick!'

A moment later, the door swung out, and the blond man who had ben first in the line entered. Behind him came two women holding trays. The man took one of Plugger's paws and led him out while the women served the food. The coffee was excellent, and the bacon and eggs and toast and cantaloupe were delicious.

While he ate, he looked steadily at Sybil. She chattered on as if unaware of his scrutiny. She had certainly acquired a set of stainless steel nerves during her imprisonment.

After breakfast, she went into the bathroom to fix herself up for the day, as she put it. Pao and Vivienne entered. The first thing she did was to get on to her knees before him, murmuring, 'Your permission, Captain!' She kissed the head of his penis.

He did not object. When in Rome, and so on. The custom certainly beat that of kissing the hand of royalty.

Pao touched his penis with one finger, also murmuring, 'Your permission, Captain.'

That was where the power and the glory were stored, Childe thought. No wonder that Igescu and Grasatchow and Dolores del Osorojo and Magda Holyani had been unable to resist using him sexually. The Ogs were supposed to have left him alone to develop into something, according to what he had garnered from the brief conversation between Vivienne and the leader of the three who had rescued him from her.

He wondered if the two werewolves had intended to kill him, as he had thought when they attacked. Maybe they had only meant to herd him back to his prison. And when he had been jumped by that wereleopard while he was killing Igescu in his oak-log coffin, he may have just been the object of her efforts to drive him away.

It was obvious now that he was supposed to develop into a Captain. But there were a number of questions to which he required answers. For one thing, what about those abandoned cars in front of his house?

Vivienne said, 'Several years ago, we had about half of a grail in our possession. It was the result of several thousands of years

101

collecting the materials needed to make the metal. Then the Togs stole it. We pursued them and cornered the one with the grail after killing his two companions. He had run into a railroad yard to get away from us, and when he saw he could not escape, he threw the grail into a gondola full of junk. At that time, we did not know that. Later, we got the information from him.'

'I can imagine,' said Childe, closing his eyes and shuddering.

'By then, the grail and the junk had gone into a steel mill furnace. We had to do some very intense detective work, very expensive, too, and we found that that particular load had ended up as metal in a certain number of cars of a certain make and model. So . . .'

'But you did not know which cars exactly?' Childe said. He was beginning to understand.

'Luckily, they were cars which were transported to this area. We had narrowed the number to about three hundred. And so we started to steal them and leave them in front of your house. We were lucky, very lucky. Three of the cars contained traces of the metal in the grail. They activated when you went near them, but you couldn't see that because the paint hid the glow, which was extremely feeble, anyway.

'We junked the cars and had them melted in a yard by a man whom we paid well. We *strained out* the grail metal, as it were, and used the tiny bits as a detector for those other cars that contained the metal. When one bit of grail is brought close to another, both glow. We no longer had to leave cars in front of your house, because we knew exactly what group of cars contained the metal. We had to do some more bribing of authorities to get the owners' names, and it was impossible to steal all the cars.

'But we got enough to act as a seed for the growth of more metal. It is a procedure that is terribly tiring for the Captain. And it exhausts those who take part in the ceremony. But it has to be done.'

Childe did not completely understand. He asked that Pao explain everything to him. This took an hour and a half with several questions still to be asked.

Nor did he accept Pao's word that the Tocs were the evil ones and the Ogs the good. The Tocs could be evil, but if they were, they were certainly matched by the Ogs.

However, what the Ogs wanted of him was not something that he had to refuse for the good of Earth. Far from it. If he took the Ogs to their home world, he would be doing his world a vast service. He would never be rewarded by humans for his heroism. In fact, if he were to bring his deeds to their attention, he would be put into an insane asylum.

There were several disturbing things about being a Captain. One was that he could return to Earth and there arrange to transport the Tocs to their home planet, too. If the Ogs could scrap cars and make a grail, the Tocs could do the same. There were plenty of cars left for that purpose.

The Ogs must have thought of this possibility. What did they intend doing about it? He hated to ask them, because he was afraid of both the truth and of falsehood. If they meant to kill him or hold him prisoner on their world, they would not, of course, tell him so. And if he asked them about it, they would know that he would have to be killed or imprisoned. Either way, he would lose.

'It will be glorious,' Vivienne was saying. 'When the Grail is complete, then you, my Captain, can materialize all the Ogs who are wandering the face of this planet as energy complexes.'

Childe was startled, and he had thought he was beyond being surprised anymore.

'You mean that I am expected to give all your, uh, dead, new bodies?' he said.

'You will enable them to give themselves their material bodies,' she said.

'It will be a resurrection day for us,' Pao said. His slanting vulpine eyes glowed. The light from the lamp was reflected redly in them.

'And just where will this resurrection or rematerializing, or whatever you call it, take place?' Childe said.

'They will materialize in the barn behind this house,' Vivienne said. 'There is more than enough room, even with all the goodzs stacked there.

'Approximately nine hundred of them,' Pao said. 'They won't be brought into matter all at once. You can control that, Captain. Ten or twenty or so at a time, and these will be conducted out of the place into this house or into rooms in the barn.'

Theologistics of resurrection day, he thought. And am I really a sort of god?

'Will Lord Byron, my real father, be among them?' he said.

Pao said, 'Oh, no. You forget that . . .'

He did not want to continue. No wonder. Byron would be among the Tocs, who would not be materialized. And Pao must be trying to guess what Childe was contemplating. How could he avoid the conclusion that the Tocs might be the good ones, if his own father was a Toc?

'Byron was a very talented man, but a very evil man,' Pao said slowly. 'History does not reveal how evil, though there are hints. The world never knew the story behind the story, of course. If it had, it would have executed him. I am sorry to say that about your father, but it has to be said. Fortunately for you, we saved you from the Tocs.'

The implication was that they had also saved him from following the evil ways of his father.

'I have a lot of thinking to do,' Childe said, 'so I'd like to be alone. What are your plans for me today, if any?'

Pao spoke in an apologetic tone. 'The Tocs will be gathering for an attack on this house. Time is more essential than ever because of this. We were hoping that you would be quite rested by evening and ready for another Grailing.'

'See me after dinner,' he said.

Pao bowed and Vivienne started to suck his cock again, but he stopped her. 'I'll save my power,' he said.

Pao looked pleased at this, but the woman frowned and bit her lip. She turned to go, but Childe said, 'One moment, Vivienne. Last night. You know what happened? I mean, are you conscious when you, uh, come apart?'

She said, 'I must be dimly conscious. When I came to, all put together, I remembered vaguely what went on. It was like a poorly remembered dream.'

'Can you have an orgasm when you're disconnected?'

'Not that I remember. If you were getting revenge, you got a pale shade of it, just as I probably got a pale shade of orgasm.'

Childe said, 'I can understand even the weirdness of the others, since they are known in folklore and superstition. But I have never heard of your type. Was your kind ever known among humans?'

Vivienne said, 'If you're referring to my structure, to the thing in me, to my discreteness, as I call it, no. I am unique. And I am recent. I was rematerialized in 1562. I had died in 1431 AD, by present reckoning. The thing in my womb died in 1440 AD. He was my very good friend then in our public human life and in our private Og life.'

'That thing was human?'

104

'Yes. You see, when we succeeded in rematerializing in 1562, we constructed ourself in our present arrangement. We can do that within certain limits, you know. We have to conform to biological laws, but if you have great knowledge you can do things with matter that you humans would think impossible.

'We had talked about such a symbiosis as this, where we could double the intensity of our sexual activities. So we materialized with this structure. Only we made a mistake. I did, rather. I had an idea that if I could be separated into various parts, and these parts could also have a sexual life, orgasm, that is, and the parts could communicate each other's orgasms . . . well, it didn't work out that way.'

Childe wondered if he was being told the truth. It seemed too fantastic. Would anybody deliberately build herself like this? Wasn't it more likely that her enemies, the Tocs, had caught her as she and the thing were rematerializing and shaped her like this? He did not know why they would do it, but it was more probable that someone would do this to another for a sadistic joke than that anyone would purposefully do it to herself.

'Both of us had very traumatic experiences in our 15th century lives,' she was saying. 'He was hung and burned at the same time, and I was burned at the stake.'

'You were a witch?' Childe said. 'Then all the witches burned were not innocent?'

'Oh, no! I wasn't innocent, but I was not a witch in the sense that my executioners thought. It was the English that burned me, you know.'

'No, I didn't know,' he said. 'Who were you? Anybody I might know?'

'I think so,' she said. 'I was Joan of Arc. And the being in my womb was Gilles de Rais.'

# 19

After the two Ogs had left, Childe lay down on the bed. Sybil had heard only the last five minutes, so he went over the entire conversation with her. She said, 'I always thought Joan of Arc was unjustly burned by the English, that she had been proved innocent of the charge of witchcraft?'

'She was condemned by the Church, but it was the Church that later removed the charge and then canonized her. I think that that happened because she was too big a hero to the French.'

'I don't understand,' Sybil said. 'What was Vivienne, or Joan, or whatever she was, doing? Why would an Og try to save France from the English?'

'Maybe for herself. Who knows what she intended to do after she had saved the nation for the French ruler? It's possible that she meant to take over from him or perhaps to control France through him. She may even have intended to drive the English out and then invade England and bring both nations under one ruler again. I didn't ask her what she and de Rais meant to do. But I'll have a chance later on. Just now, I'm too stunned.'

'Who was Gilles de Rais?'

'He was a Grand Marshal of France, one of the best warriors and generals the French had. He was also savagely sadistic, a psychotic homosexual who abducted, tortured, mutilated, and sacrificed hundreds of little boys. Little girls, too, I think. A member of the royalty or the nobility could get away with a lot in those days, but he went too far. He was charged with witchcraft, ritual murder, and a number of other things, including sodomy, I think. He was executed and quite properly, too. Few people have ever been so bestial. He made Jack the Ripper look like a gentle old fuddyduddy.'

Sybil shuddered but did not say anything. He got off the bed and undressed while she looked wide-eyed at him.

'Take your clothes off,' he said.

'Why?'

'Because I want to make love to you. Is that surprising?'

'Yes, it is, after last night,' she said.

She started to unbutton her blouse and then stopped.

'Aren't you supposed to save yourself for tonight?'

'Here, I'll help you undress,' he said.

He began to unbutton her.

'Yes, I am. But what they want and what I want do not necessarily coincide. Besides, if I'm dry, what can they do about it?'

'Oh, no! You shouldn't do that!'

'Whose side are you on?'

'Well, yours, of course! But I don't want them to get mad at you, Herald. Or at me.'

'You can always tell them I made you,' he said, grinning. 'In more senses than one.'

'I really shouldn't,' she said, staring at his slightly swelled cock.

'Go ahead. Touch it.'

'I'm not an Og,' Sybil replied. 'But if you say so.'

He stripped her blouse and unhooked her bra and took it off. She had full well-shaped breasts that had not yet begun to sag. He kissed the nipples and saw them swell and then he sucked on both, one after the other. She stood against him, her back slightly arched, and moaned. She reached down and tenderly fondled the shaft of his cock, which was expanding with his kissing and her caressing. He kissed her breasts all over and then backed her towards the bed, where he eased her down. He removed her skirt and her panties, and moved in between her legs. The thick black fleece of her cunt was beginning to run; she had always overlubricated. He licked along the slit, putting the tip of his tongue in between the lips and running it up and down. Then he pressed the tip against the clitoris, ran it back and forth, and inserted two fingers into her slit and moved them slowly back and forth and then more swiftly. She came finally with a fierce deep groan and pulled on the hairs of his head.

After this, he came up from between her legs and slid on up by her. He pushed her head down towards his penis, which was sticking up straight and hard and swollen. The head was purple, glistening, and the skin was stretched so tight it seemed about ready to burst. The blue veins stood out like unmined mineral under the reddish skin.

Sybil sucked on his testicles a while, one after the other, while she ran a finger partway up his anus. He moaned with the delight of the mouth and tongue and the finger. Then she ran her tongue lightly along the shaft of his peter, wet his pubic hairs with her tongue, and took the big head into her lips. Her tongue trembled on the slit of the glans, and her lips moved noisily with their sucking. The edges of her teeth brushed against the tight tender skin.

He blew into her mouth with a writhing of belly muscles and hips and a feeling of flying apart.

Sybil continued to suck, having swallowed the fluid. She worked at him, occasionally stopping to murmur endearing words. His dong began to rise again and when it was fully rigid, he told her to lie down. He got down on top of her and eased his prick into the slit until the pubic hairs were crushing each other. He lay there for some time, luxuriating in the warmth and the moisture and the tenderness. Her sphincter muscle squeezed on his cock, gently working it.

'I'm no superman, you know, Sybil,' he said. 'Once or twice a night, and I'm done for, usually. But when I was at Igescu's that hog of a woman, Grasatchow, put a suppository up my rectum that acted as an aphrodisiac and an energy source. And last night they gave me a drink that had the same effect. Maybe some of that effect is still with me, which is why I could get a hard-on so quickly after coming. Or maybe it's just because I've been so long without you, and you're my aphrodisiac. Anyway, I love you, and I intend to fuck all day.'

'I love you, too,' Sybil panted. 'Do you want to move now, Herald?'

He began to thrust, slowly at first and then more swiftly as he felt the tide in him increasing its forward swings. He came with a moan at the same time that she screamed with ecstasy. Tears rolled down her face on to the pillow.

His speculation that the drug he had taken was still affecting him was probably true. He lost some rigidity after the shooting out of his sperm, but he kept his peter in her, and within a minute or two it was rigid and apparently ready to tap on new reserves.

However, this time, the gray liquid in him would not rise so soon. He hammered her for what seemed like fifteen minutes and though the ecstasy built up, he could not come. Sybil was having one orgasm after another. Her eyes were open and her hands were flung out and she was rolling her head back and forth and groaning and weeping.

Suddenly, she gave a scream and seemed to fall unconscious. He was not worried, since she had behaved like this frequently. When she had an especially exquisite orgasm, she would faint.

But the white body beneath him became reddish. The smooth but wet-slippery skin was covered with hairs as red as an Irish setter's and as wet as if it had just climbed out of the water. The face became elongated and snouted, the long head hairs shrank to a bristle, the eyes shifted towards the sides of the head, the small and delicate ears became large hairy pointed organs.

The long-fingered well-manicured hands became paws with blunt hooked nails. The legs on his shoulders became hairy, and a big hard penis was against his body. It was spurting gism over his belly and down on to his own cock, which was buried to the hairs in the hairy anus of the creature.

It was too late for him to stop. He had been on the verge of ejaculating as the metamorphosis took place. Moreover, he had suspected that this thing was not Sybil. She had been too blasé about the change of shape of Plugger, too calm about what was happening, and too eager to fuck him. Sybil might have wanted to fuck him, but she would have been too afraid of emptying him and so making their captors angry. This thing should have been afraid of that, too, and probably had been, but it could not resist the temptation to get the power and the glory of the Captain's cock all to herself.

That had been the thing's undoing. It had become overwhelmed and had lost control. Apparently, it still was not aware of this.

He exploded inside the red-haired ass of the creature. The intensity of the orgasm was such that, afterwards, he felt almost forgiving. Almost but not quite.

Panting, he lay for a while on top of the wet and hairy body.

Then he got off the bed and seized its neck between his hands. It was as tall and almost as heavy as he, but it was terrified. Its brown eyes bulged out as its air was squeezed off, and its paws flailed.

Childe turned, swinging it off its feet, and then dragged it by its ears to the door. He shouted until the door was opened and then he shoved the thing out with a kick just under its long bushy tail. The three who received it looked shocked.

'That'll be the last trick you play on me!' he shouted. 'Where is my wife? You had better produce Sybil, and quick, or you'll get nothing out of me anymore! No matter what you do!'

The thing got off the floor, rubbing its spine with a paw, and whined. It said something, but the shape of the mouth was not appropriate for human speech.

'Kill it!' Childe shouted. 'Kill it and prove to me that you did! And then bring me Sybil, my wife, alive and well!'

The door swung inwards and locked. He raged around the room for a while. Finally, he burst into tears and wept for a long time. Then he got up and took a shower and dressed again. Pao and the big Swedish-type blond, O'Brien, entered.

# 20

At nine that evening, Forry Ackerman and four Tocs, including Alys Merrie, set out for their rendezvous. Forry had had to exercise his imagination to the rupture point to explain to Wendy why he wasn't going to the monthly soiree with her and to the host and hostess why he couldn't make it. He didn't think he satisfied anybody with his excuses, but certainly they were far more satisfactory than the truth.

The rain had stopped for several hours after five o'clock, and some of the clouds overhead thinned out. Then darkness and lightning had moved back in and thunder had come. A half hour later, it began raining savagely.

Every channel was filled with news of the damage done by the floods and the lives lost. The radio seemed to talk of little else, between bursts of rock music. Over two thousand homes had had to be abandoned. At least that number were in danger of sliding down a hill or being floated away. Most of the canyons were closed even to those who lived in them. The rivulets and brooks roaring down from the hills had become small rivers and frightening tidewaters. The Basin and the San Fernando Valley were sometimes knee-deep in water. Business was at a standstill; most of the bus lines had quit running. The governor had finally declared the three counties a disaster area. Citizens were screaming about flood control, and an insurance man was gunned down by an enraged citizen who had lost his home under an avalanche of mud.

The grocery stores were beginning to run short of supplies. There was water contamination and a backing up of the sewers. Despite the almost continuous rains, fires were numerous, and one fire truck, answering the twentieth call that day, dropped into a tremendous hole created by the torrents slamming down from the hills. No one was drowned, but the truck was lost.

Just before he left, Forry received a call from Wendy. The party had been called off, even though most of the guests lived within a few miles of the house where the monthly party of science-fiction people and normals was being held. It should have been cancelled days before, but the hostess was unusually stubborn.

He sighed with relief. Telling the lies had burdened him down, and at the same time he resented the burden. Why should he worry about breaking an engagement for a party when the fate of the world depended on what he and the Tocs did tonight? Nevertheless, he did worry.

Hindarf drove a pickup truck which was several times in water higher than the wheels. At Sunset and Beverly Drive, he pulled to the curb. A semi with a big van came along five minutes later and stopped with a hissing of air brakes. They got down out of the pickup and waded through water up to their ankles to the van. They had to hold on to each other to keep from being swept off their feet by the current. A piece of timber, which looked as if it had been a post for a billboard, swept by them. If it had struck a leg, it would have cracked the bone.

There were twenty others in the van. The back doors were closed, and the truck pulled away. With its high body and its power, it should get through water which would down out an automobile.

On the way, Hindarf gave them instructions. Apparently, everybody except Forry had heard these before, but he was making sure that they understood them. The instructions took about fifteen minutes, and the putting on of the diving suits, flippers, tanks and goggles about ten. Forry objected that he had never been scuba diving but was told that he would be underwater for only a minute. The main reason they were wearing the suits was to keep from getting cold while they went through the water.

The truck stopped on a steep slope. The doors were opened and a small ladder let down for Forry while the others leaped out on to the road. They were parked on Topanga Canyon just outside the entrance to the road that ran up to the house of the Ogs. The brown flood running off it joined the ankle-deep current coming down Topanga. Forry was glad that he wore flippers and a suit and that the tank gave him more weight to resist the current. But he did not think that he could carry it up the hill.

'Sure you can,' Hindarf said. 'Put on the goggles and start breathing through the mouthpiece.'

'Now?' Forry said.

'Now.'

Forry did so, and at the first breath he felt more energetic than at any time in his life since he had been a child. The air filled his whole body with a strength and a *joie de vivre* that made him want to sing This was impossible, of course, with the piece in his mouth.

112

Hindarf said, 'We may have a hard fight ahead. The vaporized drug in the breathing system will charge our bodies. The effect is intense but short-lived.'

They walked up the road, their flippers slop-slopping. They looked like Venusians, Forry thought, what with the frog feet, the slick black skins of the suits, the humped air tanks, the goggles, and the big mouthpieces. Some even carried tridents or fishing spears. The rain fell heavily on them, and everything was dark and wet, as if they were under the clouds on the nightside of the second planet from the sun.

Before they came to the turn of the road that would have placed them in view of those in the house, they started to climb the hillside. This was steep and muddy, and they could only get up by grabbing bushes and pulling themselves up. He appreciated the suit now, since it kept him from getting wet and muddy. The weight of the tank seemed negligible, so strong did he feel. His heart was chugging along at its accustomed pace, which meant that the extra demand for energy was being taken care of by the drug in the air system.

After slipping and sliding and hanging on to the bushes, they crawled out on to the top of the hill. Another hill to their right hid them from view of those in the house, although Forry did not understand how they could be seen in the dark.

Hindarf led them around the larger hill and up to a high brick wall. This was topped by a barbed wire fence about three feet high. Several Tocs unfolded a ladder, a stile, really, and put it over the wall and the wire fence. Hindarf cautioned everybody not to touch the wires, which were charged with high voltage. One by one, they crawled up the stile and over the wall and down to the other side.

They were in an orchard which seemed to run several hundred yards north and south from where they stood and an indeterminate distance west. The stile was taken down, telescoped, and placed under some bushes. Hindarf led them through the trees until they came to another slope. This rose steeply to a low brick wall. There was a flight of steps made of some stone which glowed red and black in the light that Hindarf and others flashed on it.

Forry had been upset by their careless use of this light, but Hindarf assured him that it was a form of black light. Forry could see it simply because his goggles had a specially prepared glass. Hindarf doubted that the Ogs had anything which could detect this form of illumination.

113

When they got to the top of the steps, they could see the black bulk of the house about fifty yards away. It was dark except for a slit of light. They went on and then were at the end of a long swimming pool. This was brimming over, flooding the cement walks, the patio, the yard, and running down the steps up which they had just climbed.

Hindarf gave Forry his instructions again and then went down into the pool via the steel ladder. The man assigned to watch Forry led him into the pool. For a moment, everything was black, and he had no idea which was up or down, north or south. Then a light flooded the area around him, and he could see his guide just ahead of him, holding the lamp. Hindarf's flippers were visible just ahead of the globe of illumination.

They swam the sixty-yard-long pool underwater as near the floor as they could get. Forry caught a glimpse of strange figures painted on the cement floor. Griffins, werewolves metamorphosing from men to beasts, a legless dragon, a penis-beaked flipper-winged rooster, a devilfish with a shaven cunt for a mouth, a malignant-faced crab being ridden by a nude woman with fish heads for breasts, and something huge and shadowy and all the more sinister for being so amorphous.

Then they were at the deep end of the pool, and Hindarf and his guide were removing a plate from the wall. It looked like any other section of the wall, but it was thin and wide and its removal exposed a large dark hole. Hindarf swam into it, the guide followed, and Forry, after a moment's hesitation, and knowing that the honor of Earthlings depended upon him, swam through the hole. The tunnel had been dug out of the earth, of course, but it was walled up with many small plates screwed together. He wondered how long the Tocs had been working on this. It must have taken them years, because their time would be limited to the early hours of the morning before the sun came up.

It was possible, however, that this tunnel had been built by the Ogs as an escape route. The Tocs, having discovered it, were taking advantage of it.

He did not know how long they swam through the tunnel. It seemed like a long time. It led downward, or at least he got that impression. Then they were popping up in a chamber illuminated by a bright arc light hanging from a chain set into the cement ceiling. A ladder gave access to a platform at the end of which hung row on row of suits. Shelves held many goggles and air tanks.

His second speculation was correct. This had been made by the Ogs for escape. But then, wouldn't they have set up guards or alarms?

Hindarf explained that they could go no farther in that direction. The door in the end of the chamber was locked and triggered to alarms. So, they would go through another tunnel, which they had dug and walled themselves.

They dived again, and Forry plunged to the bottom of the tunnel. He saw Hindarf go through a hole which was so narrow that the air tank on his back scraped against the plates. The tunnel curved rapidly and took them on a course that he estimated would bring them about even with the ending of the Og tunnel but about forty feet westward.

He came up in another chamber, much smaller than the first. There was a raft made of wood and inflatable pontoons. It was near the wall, which held a ladder that ran to the ceiling, twelve feet up.

Hindarf pulled Forry onto the raft. A man handed Hindarf a paper in a sealed package. He opened it and took out the paper and spread it out. Under the lights they had brought, with the only sound the slight splashing of the men and heavy breathing, they studied the plates which constituted the ceiling of this chamber. The plates were being removed by two men standing on the ladder.

There was a great boom from above them.

The shock was sudden and savage. The platform rose into the air above the water and the men on it went with it. Dirt fell in on all sides, striking the men and sending up gouts of water and clunking into the raft, which was tilting to one side and then to the other.

But the walls did not fall in, though the plates were bellied out or buckled and broken here and there. The booming noise had come and gone, like an overhead explosion. All was quiet except for the loud slap-slap of the see-sawing water against the sides of the pit and the groaning of the platform moving up and down.

Hindarf was the first to break the silence. He said, 'That was either an earthquake or the house is starting to slide. In either case, we go ahead as planned. We'll be out of this place and into the house in a few seconds.'

The two men on the ladder had clung to it as it had threatened to topple over. Now they went to work and removed the plates to make a wide opening above them.

Forry wondered why they worked so slowly. He felt like clawing the plates out and anything else that stood between him and the open air. But he managed to subdue the panic. After all, as he had already told himself, he was upholding the honor of Earthlings.

Hindarf climbed the ladder and began to chip away at the dirt with a small pick. Forry moved to one side to avoid the falling matter, which came down in big chunks. His guide, pointing at the diagram, said, 'We are directly below the floor of the room where Childe should be held.'

'How did you get hold of the diagram?' Forry said.

'From the city archives. The Ogs thought that they had removed all of the plans of the house, which was built long ago. But there was one plan which had been misfiled. We paid for a very expensive research, but it was worth it.'

'Why do you think Childe is in the room above?'

'The Ogs have held important prisoners there before, both Toc and Earthling. We could be wrong, but even so we'll be inside the house.'

Hindarf quit scraping away the dirt and was listening through a device, one end of which was placed against the stone. Then he put the device in a pocket and pouch of his suit and began to work on the stone with a drill. Forry listened carefully but could hear no sound from it. His guide told him that it used supersonic waves.

The removal of several blocks of stone took some time. Hindarf and another man stood side by side on the narrow ladder and eased each block down between them, and this was passed slowly between the men standing together on the ladder.

Then Hindarf listened again. He looked puzzled as he put the device away.

'There's a strange swishing and splashing noise,' he whispered.

He took the large square of metal which a man handed him and screwed it to the underside of the floor. A wire led from one side of the metal square to a small black metal box held by a man on the raft.

Everybody except Hindarf got off the ladder and stood to one side. Hindarf nodded to the man holding the box, who pressed a button on its top.

The metal square and the section of floor within it fell down past Hindarf.

A solid column of water roared through the opening. It knocked

Hindarf off the ladder, struck the small platform, sprayed out over the raft, and swept those standing on the platform into the well or onto the raft.

Forry Ackerman was one of those swept off.

# 21

Pao said, 'Your wife died three months ago.'

'You killed her!' Childe raged. 'You killed her! Did you torture her before you killed her?'

'No,' Pao said. 'We did not want to hurt her, because we meant to bring her to you when you were ready for us. But she died.'

'How?'

'It was an accident. Vivienne and Plugger and your wife were forming a triangle. Plugger was stimulating Vivienne with his tongue in her mouth, your wife was being stimulated with Plugger's cock in her mouth, and Vivienne and your wife had their cunts almost touching each other, face to face as it were. Gilles was up your wife's cunt or alternating between her cunt and her asshole, I believe.'

'I can believe that Sybil might engage in some daisy chains,' Childe said. 'But I can't believe that she'd let Vivienne even get near her. That snake-thing would horrify her.'

'When Plugger is charging you, you get excited enough to do a lot of things you wouldn't otherwise do,' Pao said. 'I have no reason to lie to you. The truth is that Gilles was driven out of his mind – he doesn't have much, anyway, just a piece of brain tissue in that little skull, he doesn't even know his own name and his talking is automatic and unintelligible even to him . . . Anyway, he went out of his head, too stimulated by Plugger, I suppose, and bit your wife's rectum. He tore out some blood vessels, and she bled to death. She kept moving and responding to Plugger's electric discharges even after she died, which was why neither Plugger nor Vivienne knew what was going on.'

Childe felt sick. He sat down on the edge of the bed, his head bent. Pao stood silently.

After a few minutes, Childe looked up at Pao. The man's face was smooth and expressionless. His yellow skin, thin-lipped down drooping mouth, thin curved nose, high cheek-bones, slanting black eyes, and black hair with its widow's peak made him look like a smooth-shaven Fu Manchu. Yet the man – the Og, rather – must be very anxious behind that glossy sinister face. He could not use the usual methods to force cooperation from Childe. Even the worst of tortures could not extract the power for Grailing or star voyaging from a Captain. Under pain, the Captain was incapable of performing his duties.

Childe thought of Vivienne, Plugger, Gilles de Rais, and the creature that had metamorphosed itself to look like Sybil. What was its name? Breughel?

O'Brien had left. Had he gone out to obey Childe and to kill Breughel?

Pao swallowed and said, 'What can I do to make this up to you?'

What he meant was, 'What kind of revenge do you wish?' And he was thinking, must be thinking, that Childe would hold him responsible for Sybil's death.

Childe said, 'I only require that the snake-thing be killed.'

Pao looked relieved, but he said, 'Vivienne will die, too!'

Childe bit his lip. The revenge he was planning did not involve killing anybody except the snake-thing, and that thing could not be called an entity. Not a sentient entity, anyway. He wanted that thing killed, but he wanted Vivienne alive to appreciate what had happened to her and the other Ogs.

'Bring Vivienne in,' he said.

Pao left and a few minutes later returned with Vivienne behind him. O'Brien and several others also entered.

'I need a butcher's cleaver and bandages and ointment and morphine,' Childe said.

Vivienne turned pale. She alone seemed to grasp what he intended to do.

'Oh, yes, and bring a wooden stool and a pair of long pliers,' he said.

Trembling, Vivienne sat down in a chair.

'Stand up and take your clothes off,' Childe said.

She rose and slowly removed her clothing.

'Now you can sit down there,' he said.

O'Brien returned with the tools ordered.

Childe said , 'I saw the film where you bit off Colben's cock with your false iron teeth. So don't plead with me.'

'I am not pleading,' she said. 'However, it was not I who bit his cock off.'

119

'I won't argue. You are capable of doing it; you probably have done that, and far worse, to others.'

He wished that she would weep and beg. But she was very dignified and very brave. What else could you expect from the woman who had once been Joan of Arc?

'Hold on to her,' he said to the others. 'Spread her legs out.'

Pao and O'Brien pulled her legs apart. They were beautiful, absolutely perfect legs, with flawless white skin. The bush on the mound of Venus was thick and auburn. She probably had the most attractive pussy that he had ever seen. There was no hint of the horror that lived coiled inside it.

Childe felt like ordering one of the men to take the next step, but if he had the guts to order this, then he felt obliged to have the guts to do it himself.

Carefully, he inserted the pliers. Vivienne started and began quivering, but she did not cry out.

He pushed the pliers in and felt around. His original intention to close the jaws of the pliers around the head now seemed foolish. He could not get them open enough, and that thing was too active. But he could drive it out, and he did.

Its wet, black-haired and black-bearded head shot out past the pliers handles. Its tiny mouth was open, exposing the sharp teeth. Its forked tongue flickered at him.

With his left hand, he caught it behind the head. He pulled it out slowly as it writhed and then placed the head and a part of the body on the stool.

Pao sucked in his breath. Apparently, up to that moment, he had expected Childe to yank the thing out by its uterine roots and so disconnect the parts of Vivienne again.

Childe said, 'Hand me that cleaver.'

Vivienne watched him take the chopper. She did not blink.

'Inject the proper amount of morphine in her,' Childe said to O'Brien. 'You do know how to do it, don't you?'

'I do,' O'Brien said. 'You have recognized me as a doctor, obviously. But this morphine will do no good. She is resistant to it.'

'I don't want to inflict physical pain on her,' Childe said. 'As little as possible, anyway. What kind of anesthetic do you have? I do want her to see this. She is not to be unconscious.'

'Never mind that!' Vivienne said. 'Get it over with! I want to feel the parting in its fullest!'

He did not ask her what she meant by that. He looked down at the snake-thing, which twisted and hissed. Then he raised the cleaver and brought it down hard across the flexible spine.

Blood spurted out across the room. The head rolled off the stool and fell on the floor. Pao picked it up and put it beside the still bleeding trunk. The head moved its mouth several times, and its eyes glared up at Childe as if wishing him evil even after its death. Then the eyes glazed, and the lips ceased to work.

Vivienne had turned gray. Her eyelids were open, but her eyes had rolled up to expose only the whites.

O'Brien smeared an ointment over the amputation. The blood quit flowing entirely. Probably, that ointment was not known to Earth doctors nor used by O'Brien in his Beverly Hills practice.

O'Brien bandaged up the body, and Vivienne was carried out on the chair. The snake body dangled down and scraped against the floor until one of the men coiled it up in her lap.

Two women came in and began to clean up the mess. Pao said, 'What shall we do with the head?'

'Put it down the garbage disposal.'

Pao said, 'Very well. Will you be ready for the ceremony tonight?'

'I'll try,' Childe said. 'Of course, Breughel emptied me.'

'Breughel maintains that you asked him to go to bed with you,' Pao said.

'I would think that his duty would have been to find some excuse for putting me off. He knew that I should be full again for tonight.'

'That is true, but the temptation is very great. And you did ask for what you got. However, if you require it, Breughel will be killed.'

'Let him live,' Childe said. 'Now, if you don't mind, I would like privacy. Complete privacy. Turn off everything, except the intercom, of course. Don't bring me anything to eat until I ask for it. I want to meditate and possibly to sleep later on.'

'As you wish,' Pao said.

Childe sat on a chair for a while. He had considered doing what the Ogs wished up to the point of taking them to their home planet. Then he had intended to land them on some other planet. Maroon them. They would find themselves on a world which could support life but would offer them little except hardship. And he would go on.

Pao had explained some of the results of the Grailing, and he knew that during the voyaging ceremony he would be able to scan through a part of the cosmos. He did not know how he could do this, but he had been assured by Pao that it was open to him. The implication was that he could go to any world he was able to see during the ceremony because the power would make him courageous.

But now, he had changed his mind. He wanted to escape. He had to get out and away. The chopping off of the snake-thing's head had sickened him. He was becoming an Og by association with them. If he continued with them, he might end up as cold and cruel as they. He had to get out.

An hour passed. Then, knowing that he did not have too much time to carry out the plan he had conceived, he arose. He went into the bathroom and turned on all the faucets. He used a nailfile to unscrew the grate over the shower drain, and he stuffed the drain with sheets. He put the plugs in the bathtub and washbasin drains. Then he looked around for weapons and tools. The Ogs had taken the pliers and the cleaver.

The nearest thing to a weapon was the jade statuette, which he could use for a club. He could also use it to listen in on anything on the intercommunication system, since it operated without wires.

He prowled around, looking for other useful items and could find none. Then he sat down on the bed and waited. It would take a long time for the water to fill the room as high as the canopy on top of the bed. He would be on top of it when it occurred, since he had determined that the canopy would support him.

The hours passed. The water flowed out of the bathroom and spread over the bedroom floor. It rose agonizingly slowly. But the time came when he had to climb up on the canopy and wait there.

The statuette in his hand spoke. 'Captain, it is dinner time. Do you wish anything to eat?'

'Not now!' he said. He gauged when the water would rise to the level of the canopy. 'In about an hour. I'll take the same food as last night! Oh, by the way, when does the ceremony start?'

There was a pause and then a voice said, 'About nine, Captain. Or later if you prefer.'

'I think I'll sleep a little now,' he said. 'Be sure to wake me about ten minutes before you bring dinner in.'

When the water lapped at the canopy, and wet his rear through the cloth, he swam out into the room. The door to the bathroom was almost under by then. He dived through the door and came up to the airpocket between the bathroom ceiling and the surface. Then he

122

dived down again. The ceiling light was still on, so he could see somewhat in the clear water. He turned off all the faucets in one dive and then returned to the top. Another dive through the door, and he swam back to the canopy.

As he pulled himself on to it, he felt a shock. The water slipped to one side of the room, as if the house had been tilted, and then it rushed back.

For a moment the motion confused him. He was panicked. What the hell had happened?

The voice said, 'Captain! If you felt that lurch, do not be alarmed! It's not an earthquake! We think that the front of the hill gave way! We're inspecting the damage now! But do not be alarmed! The house is at least forty feet from the edge of the hill!'

Everybody in this house was so engrossed in the Grailing that they had forgotten about the deluge and its possible effects. Other houses were slipping and sliding, tumbling down hills which caved out from under them. But these people had felt themselves insulated from the disaster. They had far more important matters to attend to.

Now was his best chance. If a large number of them were out of the house, looking at the slide, he had a clearer road out than he had hoped for.

He spoke into the statuette: 'I'll take my dinner right now.'

'Sir,' said a voice. 'It isn't ready yet.'

'Well, send a man in. The slide broke a water pipe in here. It's flooding my room.'

'Yes, sir.'

He waited. He had slipped the statuette between his belt and his stomach. He poised now, hoping that the pressure of the water would spring the door outwards even more swiftly than it normally traveled.

The caving in of the hill front had undoubtedly been the main factor in making the house lurch. But the enormous weight of all the water in this room had helped. Now, if only things worked right.

Suddenly, the door swung out. There was a yell, cut off by the roar of the water pouring out through the door. The water churned and frothed as it fought to get through the narrow exit.

Childe hesitated several seconds and then he dived. He was caught by the current and hurled through the doorway, brushing it as he went by and hurting his ribs and hips. He smashed into the wall on the side of the corridor opposite the door and then was shot, turning over and over, helplessly down the hall. The house must have been tilted slightly forward, towards the road, when it had shifted in response to the cave-in. Most of the flood seemed to be charging in that direction.

# 22

The water fell through the hole in the floor as if it were a waterspout. It pounded the narrow platform, making it shudder and threaten to break up. It swirled the raft around so that several men in the water, clinging to the side of the raft, were crushed between raft and wall.

Forry, hanging on to another man on the raft, thought that this time the house had slipped forward after another cave-in. This time, it was not going to stop. It would go down the hill, and everybody in it would be buried under tons of mud. Especially those in this underground hole!

The worst part of it was that they had removed their air tanks and so could not swim back through the tunnel.

Or could they? It was difficult to think coherently while the water was roaring through that hole and the raft was spinning and he could not see much because of the splashing and spraying around him. But it had seemed to him that the swim through the tunnel was a very short one and that he would not have to swim under the surface of the swimming pool to its end. He could emerge at once.

But the thought of going through the curving tube when its side might collapse at any second unnerved him. Bad as it was being shut in this hole here, he would stay.

By then all the lights had been extinguished, and he was in total darkness.

Suddenly, though the raft was still turning, the turbulence was much reduced. A light came on, and he could see another light. This was shining down through the hole in the floor. Water was still coming through but it was a trickle compared to the first discharge.

Hindarf was shouting at them to be quiet. Miraculously, he was unhurt.

Under his directions they erected the ladder again, and he climbed on up through it. His men followed him. Presently, a man pushed Forry and urged him to get going. Forry scrambled up the ladder swiftly but reluctantly. He poked his head through the floor and saw a bedroom that had been submerged only a few minutes before. The only exit was blocked with chairs, tables, and a bed, which had been swept against the doorway by the current.

The Tocs worked furiously to clear the furniture away. Hindarf and another looked for Childe, but he was not in the room.

'What happened?' Forry said to Hindarf.

'I don't know. But I would guess that Childe or whoever was a prisoner in here flooded this place. When the door was opened, he went out, riding the waters. He may have escaped.'

'Good!' said Forry. 'Maybe we can leave then?'

Hindarf looked down the hall at the wreckage. Several tables and vases and a crumpled carpet were piled at the corner where the hall turned. Part of the wall, where the water had first struck, was broken in. A man with a broken neck lay against the wall. He was identified as Glinch, an Og who had once terrorized medieval Germany as a werewolf. For the past twenty years, he had been working in the Internal Revenue Service, Los Angeles.

Hindarf gave direct orders. Part of the Tocs were to go down the hall, looking for whatever they could find in the way of Childe, the Toc prisoners, and the Grail. He, Ackerman, and the rest of the party would go in the other direction.

As they split up, they were hurled off their feet by another shock. Somewhere in the house, a great splintering and crashing sounded.

'We may not have much time left!' Hindarf said. 'Quickly!'

They broke in a door which was jammed because of the twisted walls. They found the three Tocs, naked, hungry, and scared, in that room. The next room contained Vivienne, whom everybody except Forry recognized. She was lying in bed, moaning with pain, a sheet over her. Hindarf pulled off the sheet, and Forry's eyes bulged. A three and a half foot long penis with an amputated head was lying between her legs, its other end stuck into her cunt.

'So somebody killed Gilles de Rais at last?' Hindarf said.

'Childe did it,' Vivienne moaned.

'Where is he?'

She groaned and shook her head. Hindarf reached out and gave a savage yank on the thing between her legs. What happened next was something that Forry would never be able to forget.

Hindarf picked up the many-legged cunt and smashed it against the wall. 'Here's something for your collection,' he said, handing the head with its kicking legs to Forry by the hair. Forry backed away and then ran out of the room.

There were shouts and then shots and screams somewhere in the house. Hindarf pushed past him and ran down the hall. Forry followed the others and eventually entered an enormous room where about twelve Tocs were struggling with ten Ogs. In the middle of the battle was a glass cube with a dully glowing gray goblet on a pedestal.

A Toc shoved the cube with his foot, and the enclosure fell with a crash, taking the pedestal and the goblet with it. There was a desperate scramble, during which the floor suddenly tilted with a deafening crash of rending timbers from nearby. The cube slid down to one end of the room while the combatants, knocked off their feet, chuted after it.

Forry was knocked down and sent sliding on his face for perhaps ten feet. He suffered friction burns on his hands and knees, but he did not notice them at that moment. The goblet had tumbled out of the cube and come to rest a foot before his face.

'Get it and run!' Hindarf yelled, and then an Og woman, whom he recognized as Panchita Pocyotl, leaped upon Hindarf from behind and bore him to the floor.

Forry would not have touched the goblet if he had thought about the effects of his act. But, excited and impelled by the Toc's order, he scrambled to his feet, scooping the goblet up. Even in his frenzied state, he noticed that it felt extraordinarily warm and that it seemed to pulse faintly. He also felt a resurgence of energy and an onslaught of courage.

He ran, even though he was not supposed to run. He went out of the room and down the hall and then there was a terrible grinding noise, a groaning, a shrieking, and a rumble as of thunder. The floor dropped; he fell, though still holding the goblet.

The room seemed to turn upside down. He struck the ceiling, which cracked open before he hit it. The lights had gone out then, but a flashlight from somewhere, maybe held by an Og who had just entered the house, threw a beam on the goblet and the surrounding area.

Half-stunned, Forry saw the goblet slide away from him. A dark figure hurtled into the area of light and sprawled after the goblet. It was not clad in a diving suit and it was not Childe, so he presumed it was an Og.

He kicked the Og as he rose with a triumphant cry, holding the goblet to his chest. The bare foot – he had long since shed his flippers – caught the Og under the cheek of his right buttock. At the same time, the house lurched again, and the Og, screaming, went flying forward. The goblet fell from his grip and rolled out through the door which was collapsing.

Cold wet mud lifted Forry and carried him as if he were on a rubber raft through the doorway just before it closed in on itself. He shot out through another room as if he were a cake of soap slipping out of the wet hands of a bather. The goblet appeared before him, riding upside down on a wave of mud. Forry reached out and grabbed it and held it to his chest even through his terror and his screaming.

Then he was turned upside down. Mud covered him and filled his nostrils and mouth. He choked and fought against the wet heavy stuff killing him.

Something struck the side of his head, and he fell into a darkness and silence blacker and quieter than the mud.

# 23

Partly stunned when he hit the wall at the first turning of the corridor, Childe was hurled down the next hall, spun off lightly at the second turning, turned aside by a great curling wave, and shot down another hall. At its end it opened on to the front door and, on the side, to a large room. The waters split here, one torrent shooting through the doorway after having broken down the door, and the other torrent spilling into the room.

The parting of the flood greatly diminished its force and its level. Childe scraped his knees and hands on the lintel as he went through the front door and was deposited at the foot of the steps at the bottom of the porch. Staggering because of the water that was falling on his back, he crawled away and then got to his feet. He took two steps and screamed as he fell outwards and down. The mud of a very steep bank took him, and he slid face down for some distance before plunging up to his shoulders into the sticky stuff. He fought his way out and then lay on his back, staring upwards.

Light was streaming out through the open door and several other windows. He was lying on top of the cave-in. And if he did not get out of the way soon, he would be crushed by the entire weight of the mansion. It was groaning and swaying, and the slides of mud around him heralded a greater slide.

Though he would have liked to stay there and rest, he turned over and slipped and slid to his feet and sludged away from the building looming above him as fast as he could go. Once he tripped over a solid object, which he would have thought was a small boulder if it had not moaned. He got down on his knees and felt the roundness, which was the head of a woman buried up to her neck.

'Who is it?' he said.

'It's me,' the woman said.

'Who?'

'Diana Rumbow. Who're you?' And then, 'Help me!'

Mud abruptly covered his legs to the ankles. He looked up but could not see much except that the house seemed to be tilting a little more. Suddenly, the lights went out, and a great grinding noise came from the house.

He went on as swiftly as he could. It would take him a long time to dig her out, and the house was surely coming down on them at any minute. Besides, he owed an Og nothing except death.

When he had gotten to one side, far enough out of danger from the house, though not from the slippage of the hill beneath him, he turned. Just as he did, the great structure screamed and toppled down the steep slope. Though it was so dark, he could still see that it had turned over on its side, so swiftly had the earth beneath it fallen in.

He wanted to make for the ruins as fast as he could, but he was too emptied and shaken. He sat down in the mud and wished that he could cry. After a while, he got up and sludged through the mud, sinking to his knees with every step. He went even more slowly than the effort accounted for, because he was never sure that he would not keep on sinking.

The first body he found was Forry Ackerman's. It was lying on top of the mud, though sinking very slowly. He was on his back, his face covered with mud but his spectacles still on. A glow of headlights coming up the road below showed him palely to Childe.

'Forry?' he said.

The mud-covered lips parted to show mud-covered teeth.

'Yeees?'

'You're alive!' Childe said. And then, 'How in hell did you get here? What's been going on?'

'Help me up,' Forry said.

Childe hauled him up, but Forry got down on his knees and started groping around. The headlights of the car came up over the top of the road below them, and Childe could see much better. But he could see nothing that Forry might be groping for.

'I had it! I had it!' Forry groaned.

'What?'

'The Grail! The Grail!'

'You had it? How? Forry, tell me, what's going on?'

Forry, feeling into the mud and cursing curses which were completely out of character for him, told him.

Childe pulled him to his feet. 'Listen, you'll never find it in this mess. We better go into the house, if we can get into that mess, and look for our friends. If they are our friends.'

Forry raised his head sharply. 'What do you mean, if they *are* our friends?'

'How much do you and I really know about the Tocs?' Childe said. 'They've been nice to us, but then they have a reason to be so. Even the Ogs became better after they had a reason to get my cooperation. So . . .'

'I have to find that Grail,' Forry said. 'I want to go to the planet of the Tocs. It'll be the only chance I'll ever have!'

'All right, Forry,' Childe said. 'We'll get it somehow. I'd like to have it, too, so I could settle this thing once and for all! But we'd better see who we can save. After all, Toc or Og, human or not, they feel pain, and they're going to need help.'

The car had approached as closely as its driver dared. Four people got out and walked through the mud to them. It took a few minutes of questioning by both parties before it was established that the newcomers were Tocs. They had been summoned from the other side of the world and had just managed to get here.

'I wouldn't worry about finding it, Captain,' the leader, Tish, said. 'You can concentrate on it, and it will glow. The glow will come up even through tons of mud.'

# 24

The Tocs and the Ogs had hired a hall.

Over two-thirds of the big dance floor of the American Legion post had been marked off in squares. The remaining third was given over to the hundred or so surviving members of both groups. And to Childe, the Captain, the Grail and its pedestal. And to Forry Ackerman, who sat on one side to observe. He would participate in the ceremony but only as one caught in the sidewash of radiation. When the time came for the voyaging, he would move into the direct influence of the power and, if all went well, travel with the others to the stars.

Childe sat in a chair before the Grail. Beyond him the Tocs and Ogs stood in ranks of twelve abreast. They were naked. Everybody in the hall was naked.

They were here because Childe had ordered it. He had told them that if both groups did not declare, and keep, a truce, he would destroy the Grail and would refuse to act as their Captain. If they agreed to keep the peace and to participate together, he would transport both groups to their home planets.

They did not take long in reaching an agreement.

Childe was still dubious about his ability to move them across intergalactic spaces and pin-point the exact world for each. But he hoped that it would work. It meant ridding the Earth of a number of monsters and potential monsters. He wished that he could do this with others than the Tocs and the Ogs.

Hindarf and Pao had died under some heavy timbers and several tons of mud. Tish had been elected master of ceremonies. It was he who had arranged that the authorities did not investigate the ruins. With the spending of much money, he had kept the police and others out of the area, and the Tocs and the Ogs who survived had secretly buried the dead.

Now Tish called up the couples, one by one, to begin the ceremony. These were male and female with each couple composed of a Toc and an Og. There were about four females left over, and these were also to couple in the beginning.

132

Male and female, they approached Childe and knelt before him. They touched his genitals and kissed his penis and then rose. He stared at the Grail while his cock became bigger with each kiss until it had reached its utmost rigidity. The Grail began to glow and to pulse. Its glow waxed and waned as the throbbings of his dong built up.

One by one they knelt and kissed or sucked his cock. Then they returned to their stations to wait, hand in hand, or hand on cock or cunt, for the last couple to return.

The light from the Grail grew brighter and brighter until it could not be looked at directly by anybody but Childe. The light filled his eyes and his skull, but he could still see the Grail and the people beyond.

Finally, Tish approached Childe and knelt and stroked his balls and cock and then kissed the glistening glans. Childe's body from behind his navel to his knees had turned to ice, and the peter was giving little jerks while the fluid moved more swiftly towards its exit. He beckoned to an exquisite Thai woman, a Toc, and she ran to him and bent over to take his cock into her mouth. Immediately, the man who had been her partner came up behind her, got down between her legs, and buried his face in her cunt. Another woman got down on all fours and began sucking his dong; a man went down on her; a woman crawled between his legs and sucked on his peter; a man thrust his tongue up her slit; a woman got under him and started to work on the head of his penis with her mouth; and so forth. The result was a daisy chain with the woman on the end lying on her back blowing a man and nobody on her cunt.

Tish walked down the line of the grunting, moaning, smacking, writhing men and women. He straddled the last woman and let himself down, not too easily, into her split.

But even while he was pumping away, Tish called out in a strange language. He chanted, and Childe understood the words, though he was not able later to translate them.

Childe sat still and let the woman mouth his glans and run her tongue over his prick while the ecstasy mounted and mounted and mounted. Suddenly, he gave a little scream and spurted. The Grail seemed to burn; it shot out a pulsing light that drove away every shadow in the hall. Tish continued to chant. Apparently, he had not come yet. And then, as Childe's peter gave its final jerk and spurt, Tish cried out.

The air over the squares darkened. Little clouds formed. The air became very cold, chilling the hot sweating bodies. There was a wind, as if the air was moving towards the clots of duskiness over each square. At first, the air moved gently, but within a minute it was whistling from every corner of the hall and rattling the windows. Dust from the floor rose up and whirled in small cyclones.

The Grail continued to pulse dazzlingly, though Childe had ceased to ejaculate. It did not obliterate the shadows above the squares; it seemed to make them darker.

The first one that Childe recognized was Igescu, the Toc whom he had killed in his oak-log coffin by thrusting a sword through his heart. Afterwards, the body had been burned to ashes in the fire of the great house.

Childe had never expected to see that long lean face with the high forehead, thick eyebrows, high cheekbones, and large eyes, nor the very long and skinny dick.

And there was Magda Holyani, the beautiful blonde weresnake.

And there was Hindarf and beside him was Pao.

They were all naked and all in their human form.

And where was Dolores del Osorojo, the beautiful California-Spanish 'ghost' who had literally fucked herself back into a materialization of flesh and blood and bone, only to be killed and skinned by the Ogs?

He saw her in a square in the middle of the crowd. She was as beautiful in her nude body as she had been in her early nineteenth century gown. She was smiling at him, and her hips were rotating as if she were relishing the memory of their times together.

The air warmed up, and the wind ceased.

The hall was filled with many voices. The living and the recently dead were chattering, yelling, laughing.

Tish waited for five minutes and then shouted for silence.

It came slowly and reluctantly, because the Tocs and the Ogs were human in that they had to express their emotions.

'Now for the voyaging!' Tish shouted.

They all faced him expectantly. Childe noted, out of the corner of his eye, Forry sitting on his chair. His eyes were bulging out, and he was covered with sweat. Childe did not know whether this reaction was caused by the ceremony he had just seen or the thought of the trip.

It was up to him whether or not he went along. If he decided to

134

go, he just had to move from the side of the hall to the middle of the floor, and he would be taken along automatically.

Tish had not liked the idea that Forry was not participating in the ceremony, but he admitted that his noninvolvement would reduce the effect of the Grail by only a negligible amount.

Tish indicated that a woman should bring up a bowl with a dark liquid in it. She took a position by Childe after kissing his penis and the second ceremony began immediately. She sprinkled his genitals with a few drops of the dark liquid before each person kissed his peter. Tish stood on the other side and every third person dipped his finger into the bowl and passed it over Childe's lips. The stuff tasted like honey with a trace of rancid cottage cheese. When the bowl was empty, Tish signaled for it to be refilled, and the ceremony went on.

The Grail kept on pulsing brightly. Its white light was beginning to affect Childe. He did not become blind or any less able to see what was going on around him. But he was receiving flashes of strange scenes. Usually these were seen as if he was standing on the surface of a planet, but several times he whizzed by a star burning redly, greenly, or amberly. He seemed to be no more than a hundred thousand miles from the great luminaries. Despite the brightness and nearness, he felt no heat, only a bone-crystallizing cold.

Tish began to chant in the foreign language. Childe beckoned to Dolores, who ran gladly towards him, her big shapely breasts bouncing with the impact of her feet. She got down on her knees and buried her face in his crotch and wept. Then she took the end of his half-limp organ and began to suck on it. It rose as if she were blowing air into it, became hard and throbbing, and gave him that first warming under his belly button.

The Grail pulsed faster, and the flickers of alien topographies and brilliantly colored stars increased in number and variety.

Dolores sucked harder and moved her head back and forth. Igescu came up behind her then and lifted her up so that she was standing up but with her knees bent. He rammed his dick into her asshole and began pumping. Plugger got down on his knees behind Igescu's buttocks, spread them, and thrust his tongue up Igescu's asshole. His body rocked back and forth as he rode the vampire's ass with his face.

Even through the woman and the man, Childe could feel the shock of Plugger's tongue. He hoped that the others would form the daisy chain quickly, because if they didn't they were going to get

135

caught short. He was going to come soon. This would require starting the voyage ceremony over again, because the chain had to be complete, or nearly complete, when he came.

The room started to rotate. The naked bodies of the men and women seemed to be skating on the edge of a spinning disc. They slid here and there, catching each other, going down, tonguing cocks and cunts, ramming cunts, mouths, and assholes.

And there was Vivienne. And there was a tall man with a black beard and burning eyes. His face had much more distinct features, of course, but the resemblance was close enough for Childe to identify him as Gilles de Rais. He had materialized in his original body, and he was sticking his dong into the spread buttocks of a slim blond man who was sucking off Vivienne.

Then Vivienne and de Rais and everybody receded on the edge of the whirling plate that had been the big ballroom. Lightning was flashing from the Grail, white strokes, scarlet flashes, emerald zigzags, yellow streaks, purple swords with jagged edges. The flashes spurted upwards from the Grail, bounced off the ceiling, spiraled down, caromed off the naked writhing bodies of the men and women, fell to the floor like colored and shattered stalactites.

Childe felt the gray fluid thrusting upward. But when he looked down, he saw only the red lips of Dolores, like an unattached cunt, squeezing around his cock. He could see into his own body, and the gray fluid was red as mercury in a thermometer and rising as if the thermometer had been thrust into a furnace. The red thread sped upward and then leaped out between the disconnected red lips and spurted like a scarlet gunpowder exploding.

The Grail blew up soundlessly with a crimson-and-yellow cloud expanding outwards and pieces of whitely glowing metal flying through the cloud.

# 25

Until the last moment, Forry could not make up his mind.

He had been repulsed at first by the orgy. Seeing such things in stag films was one thing, but seeing them in the flesh was very uncomfortable and even sickening. After a while, the aura of reeking sexuality, of uninhibited orgasms, of penises and vaginas and anuses and mouths, began to excite him. He even got jealous when he saw Alys Merrie sucking on the red-skinned cock of a big Amerindian, and he felt an impulse to get off the chair and dive into the welter, that raging sea, of hair and flesh.

But he was, in the end (I always pun, even here, he thought), too inhibited.

Nevertheless, the vibrations were getting to him, and he hoped the ceremony would not last too long. Otherwise, he might abandon his restraints and join in the fun.

A few seconds later, he got his first view of what was taking place in the mind of Childe. He did not know that it was Childe's mind that was broadcasting, but he surmised that it was. There was no doubt that Childe and the Grail, hooked together in some psychosexoneural manner, formed the focus and the distributor of the strange power emanating throughout the hall.

The glimpses of the alien worlds were like seeing the paintings of Bonestell, Paul, Sime, Finlay, St John, Bok, Emshwiller, and other greats of science-fiction become three dimensional and then become alive. Painting turned into reality.

The worlds were only slices; it was as if Childe was cutting the cosmic pie into slim pieces and hurling them at him.

He jumped up from the chair and unsteadily made his way towards the complicated shifting structure of flesh. It was only a few feet from him but it seemed to have sped towards the horizon. Between him and the bodies writhing in the glory of the power from the Grail was a vast distance.

He had to hurry. The Childe – Child? – was coming. If he did not get within that blaze, he would be left behind. He would be standing alone, naked and erect and weeping in the big American Legion hall. This was the only chance he would ever get. He, Forry Ackerman, the only human to get a ticket to intergalactic space, to alien and weirdly wonderful worlds in a foreign galaxy. His childhood dreams come true in a universe where he had no right to expect that any dreams would ever be reality. Where he had built a house to embody dreams with only half-reasonable facsimiles. Where the pseudoworlds had seemed to be real in the shadow world of his home but real for split-seconds only. Where stars like giant jewels, and crimson landscapes, and trees with tentacles, and balloon-chested Martians with elephant trunks and six fingers, and huge-eyed feathered nymphs, and long-toothed red-lipped vampires dwelt in startling fixity forever.

Now he could go voyaging.

He ran towards the dwindling figures while the Grail sent up a mushroom cloud of red, green, yellow, purple, and white shoots. He ran towards them, and they shot away as if on skates.

'Wait for me!' he cried. 'I'm going, too!'

The horizon, so distant, suddenly reversed its direction and charged him and was on him before he could stop running. Like a locomotive appearing out of a tunnel, it ran over him with flashing emerald, topaz, and ruby lights screaming at him instead of a train whistle, and swiftly rotating puffs of brilliant white and deep-space black cutting through him instead of iron wheels.

Whatever the objective length of time, to him it seemed instantaneous. He was in the hall and then he was in a huge room with gray walls, floor, and ceiling. It had no furniture and no doors or windows. The only light was that escaping in waves from the Grail.

Childe and the others were with him. They were all looking at each other dazedly. Some of them had not yet uncoupled.

The Grail and its pedestal stood before Childe.

Hindarf strode to the wall and spoke one word. A large section of the wall became transparent, and they were looking out over the bleakest landscape that he had ever seen. There was only naked twisted rock. There was no vegetation or water. Yet the sky was as blue as Earth's, indicating that there was an atmosphere outside.

Childe said, 'Come here, Forry. Take my hand.'

'Why?' Forry said, but he obeyed.

Hindarf activated another window on the opposite wall. This showed more windswept rock, but far away, near the horizon, was a spot of green and what looked like the tops of tall trees.

'This isn't our world or the Ogs' either!' Hindarf shouted. He pointed into the sky and Forry could barely see the pale moon there. It looked as large as Earth's, but it was darkly mottled in the center and resembled the markings on the wings of a death's-head moth.

Childe beckoned to Dolores del Osorojo, who smiled and came to him and stood on his left, holding his hand. Childe said something in Spanish to her, and she smiled and nodded.

'That about uses up my knowledge of Spanish,' Childe said. 'But she prefers to stay with me. And I want her to be with me.'

'That is the moon of Gruthrath!' Hindarf shouted.

He wheeled upon Childe, 'Captain! You have brought us to the desert world of Guthrath!'

Childe said, 'It's a desert, but it can support you and the Ogs quite comfortably, if you get out and dig, right?'

Hindarf turned pale. Weakly, he said, 'Yes, but surely you are not thinking of . . .?'

'My ancestral memory or genetic memory or whatever you call it has been opened,' Childe said. 'I know that there is very little chance that either you Tocs or Ogs would let me go once I made the first landing on either planet. You have Captains greater than I who could neutralize my powers long enough for your people to physically capture me. You'd have to, because I am partly an Earthman, and you could never trust me. And whichever planet I got us to first, the home of the Toc or the Og, the people there would catch me. And they would take captive the enemy peoples, too.'

'That isn't true!' Hindarf and Igescu yelled.

'I know,' Childe said. 'You two were taking a chance in a cosmic lottery, as it were. You did not know which planet I would pick out to land on first, and you couldn't even ask me, because I would not know which one until I was presented with a choice. Also, if you tried too hard to sway me, I might get suspicious. So you took a chance. And both of you lost.'

'You can't do this!'

The Tocs and the Ogs rushed towards Childe.

Forry almost let loose of Childe, because it looked as if the three of them were going to be torn to bits.

Childe gripped Forry's hand so hard that the bones cracked.

He shouted, 'Fuck you!' and they were off.

There was a thin triangle of nothing wheeling by Forry, a gush of soundless purple flame around his feet, and the familiar walls of the

139

American Legion hall were all around him and the familiar floor was under his feet.

Forry did not say anything for a moment. Then, slowly, he spoke. 'Where's the Grail?'

'I left it behind. I can do that, you know, although it means that the Grail is now forever out of my reach. Unless another Captain brings one here.'

'That's all?' Forry said. 'You mean the trip's *over?*'

'You didn't get *killed*,' Childe said.

'I made a better trip when I saw the movie *Barbarella*,' Forry said.

Childe laughed and said, 'You'd gripe if you were hung with a new rope.'

They got dressed and prepared to leave the hall. Childe said, 'I wouldn't tell anybody about this, if I were you. And I think we'd better not see each other again.'

Forry looked at Dolores. She was dressed in a white peek-a-boo blouse and tight orange slacks that one of the Toc women had left behind.

'What about her?'

Childe squeezed the dark-haired woman and said, 'I'll take care of her. She may have been one of *them*, but she was one of the good ones.'

'I hope so,' Forry said. He stuck out his hand. 'Well, good luck. *Adiau*, as we Esperantists say.'

'Don't take any wooden grails,' Childe said.

Forry watched him walk away with his arm around the slender waist of Dolores, his hand resting on the curve of her ass. How could the fellow so easily give up that power, that chance to go star-voyaging?

But he felt good again when he came out into the familiar world of Los Angeles. The rains had stopped, the night sky was clear and full of stars, car horns were blaring, water was splashing on to the pedestrians as reckless drivers roared through pools, a radio was screeching rock, an ambulance siren was wailing somewhere.

A half hour later, he entered his house. He stopped and gasped. The Stoker painting was missing again!

Lorenzo Dummock came down the steps then, scratching his hairy chest and swollen paunch. He said, 'Hi, Forry. Say, could you loan me a coupla bucks for ciggies and a beer? I'm really down in the dumps, I . . .'

140

'That painting!' Forry said, pointing his finger at the blank space on the wall.

Lorenzo stopped and gaped. Then he said, 'Oh, yeah, I was going to tell you. That guy, what's his name, Woolston Heepish? He showed up about an hour ago and said you had told him he could have the Stoker. So I let him. Wasn't it all right?'

Forry charged into his office and dialed Heepish's number. His heart chunked when he heard the smooth voice again.

'Why didn't you go with the others?' Forry said.

'Why, Forry! You're back! I thought sure you'd be gone forever! That's why I stayed behind. I like this life, and I couldn't pass up the chance to add your collection to mine!'

Forry was silent for a moment and then he said, 'Hold on! I thought you were buried in that landslide?'

Heepish chuckled. 'Not me! I was slid out as nice as pie and took off. I had enough of Childe and the Tocs and the Ogs, even if the Ogs are my people.'

'I want my painting back!'

'Would you consider trading it for a rare Bok?'

Forry wondered if the fellow had slipped some LSD into his coffee. Perhaps everything that had happened was only a lysergic acid fantasy?

Heepish's voice, fluttering like the wings of a bat in the night, said, 'Maybe we could get together soon? Have a nice talk?'

'You can keep the painting if you'll promise never to cross my path again!' Forry said.

Heepish chuckled. 'Could Dr Jekyll get rid of Mr Hyde?'

## The most chilling horror stories – now available in Panther Books

**Max Ehrlich**

| | | |
|---|---:|:-:|
| The Cult | 95p | ☐ |
| The Edict | £1.95 | ☐ |

**Mendal Johnson**

| | | |
|---|---:|:-:|
| Let's Go Play at the Adams' | £1.50 | ☐ |
| Poltergeist | £1.95 | ☐ |

**David Seltzer**

| | | |
|---|---:|:-:|
| Prophecy | £1.50 | ☐ |

**Charles Veley**

| | | |
|---|---:|:-:|
| Night Whispers | £1.95 | ☐ |

**William K Wells**

| | | |
|---|---:|:-:|
| Effigies | £1.95 | ☐ |

**Jay Anson**

| | | |
|---|---:|:-:|
| 666 | £1.50 | ☐ |

**Peter Loughran**

| | | |
|---|---:|:-:|
| Jacqui | £1.75 | ☐ |

**Brian Lumley**

| | | |
|---|---:|:-:|
| Psychomech | £1.95 | ☐ |

To order direct from the publisher just tick the titles you want and fill in the order form.

All these books are available at your local bookshop or newsagent, or can be ordered direct from the publisher.

*To order direct from the publisher just tick the titles you want and fill in the form below.*

Name _____

Address _____

_____

Send to:
**Panther Cash Sales**
**PO Box 11, Falmouth, Cornwall TR10 9EN.**

Please enclose remittance to the value of the cover price plus:

**UK** 45p for the first book, 20p for the second book plus 14p per copy for each additional book ordered to a maximum charge of £1.63.

**BFPO and Eire** 45p for the first book, 20p for the second book plus 14p per copy for the next 7 books, thereafter 8p per book.

**Overseas** 75p for the first book and 21p for each additional book.